Stargazey Nights

Stargazey Nights

A Novella

SHELLEY NOBLE

wm
WILLIAM MORROW
An Imprint of HarperCollinsPublishers

Excerpt from *Stargazey Point* copyright © 2013 by Shelley Freydont.

EPub Edition JUNE 2013 ISBN: 9780062261991

Print Edition ISBN: 978-0-06-226200-4

10 9 8 7 6 5 4 3 2 1

Stargazey Nights

Chapter 1

CAB REYNOLDS NURSED HIS SCOTCH and looked out at the nighttime skyline of Atlanta. It was his kind of skyline, modern, geometric, minimal. Like his apartment—like his life.

He could hear Bailey in his bathroom, the hum of her hair dryer, the clink of the perfume bottle against the marble countertop. She never rushed. Even when they were late. Which they were. A big celebration, the kickoff of a new project, an MPR, a master plan resort, a self-contained resort community in the middle of Myrtle Beach, South Carolina. A party of sorts. Lots of laughter, champagne with satisfied colleagues and clients.

Tomorrow night it would be a fund-raiser held by Bailey's parents. Cab took a sip from his drink and turned from the window. The smell of scotch was the last thing he remembered before Bailey came out of the bedroom and the telephone rang.

He put his drink down, tempted to ignore the phone. Bailey had that effect on him. Made his blood race and desire shoot through every part of his body. But he knew better than to muss her hair or her tiny dress or makeup when she was ready to go.

He answered the phone.

"Cabot Reynolds?"

"Yes?" Who would be calling him at eight o'clock on a Thursday night? He was on every do-not-call registry on record. The firm wouldn't give out his number, so . . .

"This is Beau Crispin . . . from Stargazey Point . . . South Carolina. Didn't mean to bother you . . ."

The slow drawl oozed on. Stargazey Point. *Stargazey Point*. Cab hadn't been there for years, but there had been a time it had been his playground, his refuge . . . his home.

"Didn't expect you to be at your office this late. I was goin' to leave a message. I don't know if you remember me or not . . ."

Beau Crispin. Of course Cab remembered him and the piece of wood he was always carving but never let anyone see. One of his Uncle Ned's best friends.

"Of course I remember you. Is anything wrong?"

"Oh, no, no. Your secretary handled everything

just fine, but Silas and Hadley and I got to talking and thought you'd want to know that everything looks real good, the casket's mighty fine, and the flowers are somethin' to behold. So you don't worry that things weren't done right. We're just sorry you won't be able to make the funeral. He would have liked that."

"What funeral?" Cab thought Beau Crispin must be crazy. He'd always been "deep," as Ned would say. But this was full-blown lunacy.

Beau Crispin was silent.

"Beau?" Cab said more calmly. "Whose funeral?"

"I'm sorry, son. It didn't occur to any of us—Your uncle died two days ago."

Ned? Died? Of all the absurdities of this conversation, Cab's only thought was, *I don't have a secretary.*

At the end of the line, Beau Crispin cleared his throat. "Well, you must be anxious to get on home, so I won't keep you."

He was home. And none of this made sense. "Don't hang up," he said quickly. He was beginning to remember Beau, really remember. And he wondered if behind the uncertainty in that old voice, he had heard just an undercurrent of censure?

Cab was vaguely aware of the bedroom door opening. Bailey's scent preceded her into the room.

"I wasn't aware. A miscommunication."

"Of course, we all understand, son. Sorry to break it to you like this."

No, you don't understand, Cab wanted to say, but *he* was beginning to.

Bailey's arm appeared before his unfocused eyes, one beautifully manicured nail pointed to the Rado watch he'd given her for Valentine's Day. She was ready to go.

He turned away from her. His uncle Ned had died. How was that possible? He couldn't be that old. Cab tried to do the math, but his brain didn't seem to be working.

The watch appeared under his nose again. This time he walked away, knowing that if he didn't get away, she would take the phone and hang up on whoever was calling. He used to think it was sexy the way she did that. Not tonight.

How had this happened? He hadn't heard from his uncle for . . . He hadn't gone to visit since—Oh God, it had been years. He meant to go, but he just hadn't found the time for the man who had been a second father to him, especially after the first one had stopped being a father at all. And he'd died without Cab's even knowing he was sick.

Bailey reached for the phone, and he wanted to slap her. And that was unfair. He held up a finger. One minute. It would piss her off. But Bailey pissed off usually led to sex. Which is where most things with Bailey led.

"Cabot? Are you all right, son?"

"Yes. Yes. Sorry. Of course. Yes. What time?"

"Two o'clock."

"I'll be there. Tomorrow. Yes."

Another of those long silences that were typical of Beau. And suddenly Cab was hurled back to his boyhood. Long, quiet sits along the seawall, with Beau trying to teach him how to carve. Fun nights at Silas's barbecue shack with Ned and Hadley and Beau. Closing up the carousel with Ned and both of them looking up at the stars. Ned saying, "There's a million wishes out there, boy. One of 'em's yours."

"You want me to call down to the Inn and tell Bethanne to fix you up a room so you'll have a place to rest and all?"

"Yes. Please."

"Cabot?"

"Yes?"

"Ned was real proud of you. Everybody will be real glad to see ya."

Cab hiccuped. "Thanks." He hung up.

"I hope whoever that was doesn't expect you to work late tomorrow," Bailey said as she took the phone from him and returned it to its base. "It's Mamma's fund-raiser auction at the Peachtree Club. She'll expect you to be there, showing your handsome self around and getting all the ladies to spend their husbands' money for a good cause."

Cab mumbled something, checked his bow tie in the foyer mirror, and helped her into her coat. He snagged his keys off the side table and opened the door. Closed it again.

Bailey's expression changed. It was subtle. It always was. Sometimes, he had to guess what it was. Tonight, he didn't care.

"Did you know that my uncle Ned had died?"

"Ned Reynolds. Why yes, they called the other day. I took care of everything."

"You took care of—"

"Honey, that's what wives of successful men do."

"Without telling me?" *She isn't even my wife yet.*

"Well, it slipped my mind. I've been so busy."

"Didn't you think I might want to go to the funeral?"

She looked mildly surprised. "Well, no. It's not like you've ever mentioned him. And I sent an enormous flower arrangement in case there was anybody there who mattered."

Mattered? They all mattered. And he must have talked about Ned with her. Hadn't he? Or had he gotten so caught up in his successful life that he'd just pushed his uncle aside. He felt humiliation roil through his stomach. And now his uncle was dead.

He wanted to kick himself for not making the trip while Ned was alive. He should have kept in touch. Introduced him to Bailey. Thanked him for all the things he had done for him. He owed the man that. Hell, he owed the man just about everything. And he'd been so full of himself, his education, his career, his life, his trophy fiancée that he'd let the most precious thing slip away unnoticed.

Bailey plucked the keys from his hand. "Stop dawdling. We're going to be late."

She stood at the door, waiting for him to open it for her. He did. Stopped to key in the security code, then walked her to the elevator.

"Don't you dare let Harold Bloomquist drag you away the minute we get there. At the last one of these, his wife talked my head off until I claimed I had to go to the loo. And for a horrifying second, I thought she was going with me. Awful creature."

Cab wasn't really listening though usually he found it fascinating that the nastier Bailey got, the sweeter her expression and the softer her accent became. It was a gift, he guessed.

Was it what wives did? Well, in Cab's case, his fiancée. Arrange funerals for an in-law-to-be she'd never met, then not tell her husband about it? He thought about his father and stepmother. It was something she might do. Not that they would be going to the funeral or sending flowers. Uncle Ned was the black sheep of the Reynolds family, something Cab's father never let him or Ned forget.

He glanced over at Bailey as they waited for the elevator.

There was no way he could drive the six and a half hours to Stargazey Point, go to the funeral, and drive back in time for the party tomorrow. But he would be going. Already, part of him was pulling him there. He had to go. It was the least he could do. And as it turned out, he hadn't done more than the minimum during Ned's lifetime. He would try to rectify that now; too little, too late. But he wouldn't tell Bailey until after the party tonight. He had enough on his plate without that.

"Well?"

The elevator doors opened, and he motioned Bailey inside. "What? Sorry?"

"I said, the wedding planner and the mater are conspiring for an antebellum wedding theme. I said absolutely not. I've already got my dress, and it requires a more sophisticated setting than some Tara revival. Really, sometimes Mother makes me wonder."

"Hmm."

"Well, don't you have an opinion?"

Cab blew out air. He didn't have an opinion. Not about venues, or color schemes, or what kind of cake to serve. Hell, it was a year and a half away. They could all get hit by a bus before then. That's what his uncle Ned had always said. Live today, you might get hit by a bus tomorrow.

"What are you smiling about? You don't have an opinion, do you?"

"Sure, I say whatever you want."

"You are so provoking."

She took his arm as they rode down the twenty-four floors to the garage. Looked up at him with those dark, sultry eyes, a playful smile on her full lips. If this had been the end of the party instead of the beginning of the evening, he knew where that expression would have led. As it was, she was just teasing him. A promise of what he could look forward to later.

And he wondered, for the first time, if he'd made the right choice.

Chapter 2

IT WAS CLOSE TO FOUR o'clock when Cab rolled his suitcase out of the apartment and set the security code. Bailey was asleep. He didn't bother to wake her before he left.

She was pretty mad. Maybe he should have told her as soon as he got the call, but then she would have been pissed all night. Frank and Tony, the two colleagues who had a real reason to be upset—there was a major financial assessment meeting tomorrow for the Myrtle Beach project—were surprised but accepting.

Already, the plans were over budget, and they hadn't even hired a bulldozer. That's the way it was when the money people thought their ideas were better than the architects'.

Frank and Tony were perfectly capable of representing Bloomquist and Ryan at the meeting without him. Bailey could handle the fund-raiser without him though she wasn't happy about it. She let him know, volatilely. He hated leaving during an argument, but she refused to understand. Or maybe she couldn't understand.

The elevator stopped, and he stepped out onto the garage level, walked past Bailey's silver Mercedes, and beeped open the hatch of his Range Rover. He lifted his suitcase into the hold and spread his suit bag over the suitcase. Closed the hatch and leaned against it, his hand resting on the closed door, his head resting on his hand.

His eyes felt gritty, and his chest hurt, lack of sleep and sadness. He'd stop someplace for coffee to remedy the first; he didn't even want to assuage the second. He laughed. The kind of laughter that came with disbelief.

"I don't think—I won't be able to get back for tomorrow night. Give your mother my apologies."

First explosion. "But everyone will be expecting you."

"Bailey, he was my uncle. I have to go to the funeral."

That caressing hand up his sleeve, the slim body pressing close to his, the soft, persuasive voice. "It's not like you know anyone there. I sent a really impressive arrangement. I'm sure they'll all understand."

Cab pushed away from the car, went around to the driver's side, and climbed in. Maybe he didn't know anyone there. Maybe the ones he had known had all moved away or died. Maybe they wouldn't remember him. But this wasn't for them or for Cab. It was for Ned. His uncle had deserved so much more.

"I have a responsibility." Something he thought she would relate to. "And I want to go."

"Oh please. The man's dead. If you cared so much about him, you should have visited him when he was alive."

"I know."

"So basically you're doing it out of guilt. Do you think any of those people care?"

"I care. And it's not just guilt though there is plenty of that. But it's about honoring his life."

Bailey's eyes rolled upward. "The man ran a merry-go-round in a backwater town. Get over it."

That's what had finally sealed it. She didn't get it at all. He'd been about to ask her to go with him. It would have meant a lot to him and to Ned and even the town that he would show that degree of respect, but he didn't bother.

"I have to go."

The change in the room temperature was decisive. "Suit yourself. I'll just tell Momma you couldn't make it." She went into the bathroom and closed the door.

Cab pulled out his suitcase and began to pack.

When she came out and went straight to bed without a word, he didn't bother to continue the conversation, just changed into slacks and sweater and left.

The wheels screeched as he drove out of the darkness of the garage and into the darkness of the street, which Cab guessed was indicative of his suppressed emotions. Not that he was sure what all of them were. But, suddenly, he was feeling a whole lot of stuff.

He drove toward the highway and pulled into a fast-food joint, ordered a large coffee and a hamburger, and headed east. Neither did much to help the acid in his stomach, but that would change when he got to Stargazey Point.

Maybe Silas was still getting up early to stoke the fires at his barbecue place. Cab's mouth watered just thinking about that hickory smell, the sweet, pungent sauce, the tender moist pork. How long had it been since he'd eaten real barbecue? He and Ned used to climb into Ned's old truck at least twice a week after the carousel closed for the night. During the season, when the carousel was open late, Beau Crispin would stop by on his way home to drop off big foil packets of food from Silas.

Cab wondered if Beau and his sister Millie still lived in their old plantation-style house on the Point. They were the biggest property owners in the area. Cab was stabbed with a sudden anxiety. He sure hoped he didn't drive into Stargazey and see the closed gates of a resort community where the old mansion had been.

And he realized that with all the reminiscing about Stargazey Point, he had no real idea of what it was like today.

He pressed down on the accelerator, as if getting there sooner would stop progress from happening. Progress that kept Cab in business and in his posh condo with an expensive girlfriend. Progress that Cab was about to initiate on an eight-block parcel of downtown Myrtle Beach. It's what he did.

But Cab wasn't a developer; he didn't build golf communities for retirees. He was an architect. A damn good one. A respected one. He built big, and unique and beautiful. Whole building complexes. Self-contained neighborhoods. Stadiums. Malls. He'd even designed a museum. He was in demand.

Still, he wouldn't want that to happen to the Point.

As he drove away from Atlanta through the sprawling suburbs, he began to feel an easing in his shoulders. As the night grew light around him, so did his spirits. And for a moment, he forgot that he was going to a funeral and just felt the pleasure of escape.

But he didn't need to escape. And Stargazey Point was no longer home. Had never really been home, except during the summers of his boyhood, after his father remarried and Cab became an afterthought except to his uncle Ned.

The Range Rover swerved, and Cab jerked the wheel, bringing it back into the lane. Maybe he had dozed off momentarily or maybe it was the realization that his stepmother might be a Boston Brahmin, but there wasn't so much difference between her and Bailey Delaney, Southern belle.

He stopped at the South Carolina border for another cup of coffee, then again for a quick breakfast on the outskirts of Myrtle Beach before turning south for the last leg of his journey. The sun was up and it promised to be a decent day. There was just the hint of fall in the air, so he wouldn't be sweltering in his suit in the unair-conditioned church. He wondered who had arranged the funeral? He should have asked Beau. Would it be in the church? Or graveside. Who would officiate? Would they expect him to say a few words?

The road cut through marshland and scrub forest, parcels of farmland dissected by gated condos. Not all were new. And many seemed to be empty. It was a different landscape than he remembered, and the closer he got to Stargazey Point, the more anxious he was to get there. It was similar to the same feeling when he was a kid though now there would be no Ned waiting with a cold Coke and a package of cheese crackers.

Cab smiled though it hurt. Simple pleasures. How he had looked forward to sitting on the front porch of Hadley's store, drinking out of the bottle and sitting with the "men." He'd felt so grown-up.

He almost passed Silas Cook's smokehouse. He slammed on the brakes and, looking over his shoulder, backed up in the road until he came to what was—had been—the best barbecue place on the whole coast.

Silas's place had never been upscale; actually, if the health department had cared, they would probably have closed him down. But those officials always came to Silas's for their barbecue, so they left him alone.

But this. The old shack was practically falling down, the roof had caved in, and the sign that had always hung over the door had half fallen to the ground. The earth in front was hard packed, but one look at the side of the building and Cab knew what had happened. The best barbecue place on the coast was going under the bulldozer.

For a moment, Cab just sat there.

Things changed. That was good. But things in Stargazey Point had changed without him, and he felt like a stranger.

He revved the engine and pulled away, throwing up gravel and dust, and when he drove into town ten minutes later, he breathed a huge sigh of relief. The buildings had a new coat of paint. There was a new art gallery, well good for them, a couple of antique stores, a real-estate office, a tea shop, Flora's. He remembered it though he and Ned didn't go there much except on special occasions. It had been given a gingham face-lift. The whole town had spruced up.

Next to the tea shop, the Stargazey Inn looked pretty much the same, a square, cream-colored building with doors and windows picked out in blue, a nod to the Gullah tradition. It had a new coat of paint, at least on the outside, but Cab suddenly wished he'd booked a real hotel back in Myrtle Beach.

But what was the point of that? He wanted to be here. Wanted to see any people he might remember. Look in at the carousel and Ned's house. So the hotel was a little old. How bad could it be?

He took his suitcase and garment bag out of the back, pushed open the white, wrought-iron gate, and walked up to the front porch. He stopped at the closed door. There was a row of rocking chairs along the porch but not a person in sight.

He opened the door—and stepped into a foyer that gave new meaning to quaint. Floral and checks and pastels covered the walls, the wicker furniture, the windows. The beds were probably soft and buried under a mound of homemade quilts.

Cab resisted a shudder and walked over to the cherrywood registration desk.

"Hello?" He dinged the bell that sat on the counter. Heard a rustling of paper, and a mousy-looking young woman hurried out of the office, wiping her hands on her skirt.

She stopped when she saw him. And her eyes widened before her mouth slowly lifted in a smile.

"Mr. Reynolds?"

"Yes. I believe Beau Crispin made a reservation for me."

"Yes, he did."

Cab opened his wallet and pulled out his Amex card.

"Oh that won't be necessary," she said is a soft drawl. "There's no charge."

"I don't . . ."

"Well, I could hardly charge you when you're Ned's nephew, now can I?"

Of course she could. She couldn't have more than six rooms if that; most landlords would have doubled the rates. Captive audience. But he would argue about it later.

"You know. I bet Ned looked just like you when he was younger. I mean, he'd gone gray. But he was still tall, and I bet his hair was dark like yours. And you definitely have his eyes. You know, most people with dark eyes look intense, and sometimes formidable. But Ned's always had a sparkle to them."

Cab suppressed a yawn. He was really tired, and this chatter was pushing him over the brink.

"Oh, listen to me prattling on. We're just so glad you could make it after all. Did you bring your fiancée?"

"No."

"Well, we'll all be sorry not to meet her. I've given you room four. It's our biggest, and it has an *en suite* bath."

Cab just bet it did, with an ancient tub and zero water pressure. "I'll only be staying tonight."

She been coming around the edge of the desk, but she stopped again. "Oh. Everybody was hoping you'd be able to stay a while."

She walked past him and picked up his suitcase.

He was so astounded he forgot to protest until she started up the stairs. What she lacked in finish, she made up in energy.

"I'll take that," he said, running to catch up to her.

"Oh, it's no trouble. We—I don't keep a bellboy during the off-season."

He cast a sideways look at her.

"Well, I never have a bellboy. But the rooms are real nice, and real clean."

She let him wrest the suitcase and bag from her.

She led the way to the second floor, to a room in back. She opened the door with a flourish, then looked anxiously at him.

The room was painted a light blue, and in the middle was a huge, four-poster bed, with some kind of white bedspread covering the mattress, which was at least three feet high. A highboy and wooden wardrobe completed the furnishings, not a closet in sight.

Just as well he and Bailey had argued. She would have demanded instant departure to the nearest four- or five-star hotel. Normally, he would, too, but the landlady was so eager to please and so obviously proud of her handiwork, he didn't have the heart to leave. Plus, he was about to fall on his face from fatigue and anxiety.

"Very nice, Ms.—"

"Mrs."

To Cab's dismay, her eyes filled with tears.

She shook them way. "Bridges, just call me Bethanne. Everybody does. There are towels in the bathroom. Anything else you need?"

"No thank you. I've been driving all night. I'd like to get a couple of hours' sleep before the funeral."

She looked at a man's watch she wore on her left arm. "You have plenty of time, the funeral isn't until two."

"And is there somewhere I can get a quick lunch before then?"

"Flora's serves sandwiches and salads and things. We only serve breakfast."

"Do you know where the funeral is?"

"It's going to be at the First Zion Baptist Church."

"He's going to be buried there?"

"He insisted on it. Said he'd been listening to them singing every Sunday that he could remember."

Cab smiled. Ned had grumbled about "that damn singing" waking him up every Sunday since he could remember.

"That's where most of his friends went, and that's where he wanted to be buried, so he wouldn't be lonely."

Cab's throat spasmed. He was afraid he might burst into tears. He hadn't done that in years. He really needed to get some sleep.

"Well, thank you Ms.—Bethanne. Until later." He gently ushered her out the door, but she turned before she left.

"We all loved Ned. He was a good man."

Cab nodded. He was a good man. And no one knew it better than Cab.

Chapter 3

SARAH DAVIS PUSHED PENNY FARLOWE out the door of Flora's Tea Shoppe.

"Careful. You're jostling the coffee and pastries," said Penny, owner, baker, and waitress of Flora's. Flora had sold out years before, but Penny kept the name. As Penny told anyone who asked, "You can't go changing the name of a place that has always been known as Flora's."

"Won't matter if you don't hurry your butt. The guy will be registered and upstairs before we get there." Sarah, barely five feet and a pencil to Penny's cushioned frame, gave her an encouraging nudge.

"Ow. I know that. But maybe we should leave the man alone. I mean, he's grieving and all."

Sarah snorted, a country habit she'd picked up since returning to Stargazey last June. "Grieving my foot. If Cabot Reynolds III were grieving, he wouldn't have had his secretary send that god-awful, nouveau riche, New Jersey big-haired flower arrangement. He would have come down to make the funeral arrangements himself. And he would have been here for the viewing."

"You sure have gotten unforgiving since you've been living up in New York with all those Yankees. Bad enough you talk just like them now." Penny moved aside to let Sarah open the gate to the Inn. "How do you know he's a third?"

"I looked him up, and I've always been unforgiving. It's one of my better traits." Sarah flashed her a smug smile and followed her up the walk. Jumped ahead to open the door. "I'm beginning to feel a little step and fetch it, doing all this work," Sarah said, relapsing into a brutal Southern accent.

Penny pushed past her. "I'd say something unladylike, but I don't want to shock Bethanne."

They bustled inside . . . to an empty foyer. Exchanged looks.

"Damn," Sarah said, just as Bethanne came down the stairs.

She saw them and put her fingers to her lips. Then she giggled. Something, Sarah realized, they hardly ever heard from the young widow. "You're too late."

Sarah huffed. "I told you we should have just grabbed a tea bag and come on over. So give us the lowdown."

Bethanne looked over her shoulder as if she thought maybe Cabot Reynolds might be afraid to stay upstairs by himself and had followed her back down. "He drove all night to get here, so he's sleeping for a couple of hours." She walked behind the registration desk.

Penny put down the plate of pastries and pulled off the plastic wrap. "We might as well eat these, seeing how he's out for the count."

"I told him he could get a quick lunch at the tea shop before the funeral."

"I'll get dressed early and meet you there," Sarah told her. "I'll even buy you lunch."

"Sarah, you're terrible."

"I know. It's because I'm bored."

Bethanne looked at her like she was crazy, which Sarah had to admit might be true. She'd given up a second year of teaching at Columbia's Cultural Studies Department to do research on the "Disappearing Gullah Culture of the Carolina Shore." Like there wasn't enough written about that already. What she was more interested in doing was recording the remnants of that culture in a real setting, with primary source material and live, on-site interviews before it disappeared altogether. So far, she hadn't had much cooperation from the locals.

At least it masked the other reason she had come back to her "roots," which was to make sure her great-grandmother was not living alone, neglected by social services, and poor.

Ervina was none of these things. She was just crazy. Or the wisewoman, depending on who you talked to.

Whatever it was, Sarah hoped to hell it didn't run in her veins. She reached for one of the lemon tarts Penny had made just that morning. "So? What does he look like?"

Bethanne shrugged. "He looked really tired."

Penny snatched the plate away. "You're as bad as Sarah. She knew him when he was young. All she said was he was a skinny white boy."

"Sarah."

Sarah shrugged. "I know, I had an aberrant moment of being un-PC." She grinned. "But it's true. That's the main thing I remember about him. And that he'd show up every summer with some god-awful version of what his folks thought was beachwear, and Ned would have to take him over to Hadley's and buy him some dungarees. And he never had his size, so The Third would go around all summer hoisting those pants up. He was the prototype of boyz 'n the hood. Only he didn't know it."

"Well, he's a lot better dressed now," Bethanne said.

"You're going to have to do better than that if you're eating my lemon tarts."

"Well, he's tall . . . and dark . . . and handsome."

Penny pushed the plate back toward her. "Girl, you've been reading too many romance novels."

"No. Really. He is. Try to imagine Ned Reynolds about forty years ago. Really dark hair. And darker eyes. Only Ned's always had a twinkle since I knew him. His nephew's eyes have a glint, but I don't think it's fun."

"Do I detect a note of interest?" Sarah knew the minute she'd said it that it was the wrong thing to say.

"Sarah, how could you say such a thing?" Bethanne's eyes filled with tears.

"Now, now, Sarah was just kidding," Penny said, patting Bethanne's arm and frowning at Sarah. "But it has been almost three years, Bethie. No one would blame you if you got interested in seeing men again."

Bethanne shook her head so vehemently that her hair swung across her face.

"Okay, whatever," Sarah said. "Call me when he's leaving for the tea shop, so I can get there in time to see him. You can come, too."

"Don't you think that would be a little obvious? Besides, you'll see him at the funeral."

"Yeah, but with all the folderol and rigmarole and 'Praise the Lords,' I might not get up close and personal."

"Why are you so interested?" Bethanne asked.

"Like I said, I'm bored. Plus, if we can guilt him out, maybe he'll give a big donation to the community center in Ned's name."

CAB WOKE TWO hours later amidst flowers and frills and thought he must have wandered into a Martha Stewart magazine in his dreams. Then he remembered. The Stargazey Inn, the mousy, sweet inn lady. This froufrou room.

He shuddered as his brain clicked in. He'd be back in his nice, sleek, urban condo tonight with any luck, but he really didn't look forward to Bailey's cold shoulder. But hell, it was his apartment. She could just be a little understanding.

He staggered to the bathroom and turned on the shower full blast. Gave the showerhead the evil eye. It had to be an antique, and the water pressure—

And he was being a goddamn, condescending ass. It was a lovely inn if you liked that kind of thing. When had he gotten so damn smug and opinionated?

The water was hot and cleansing, and he stood there, mindless, for way too long. Then he got out and dressed in his summerweight suit.

He went downstairs. He was pretty sure he remembered the church from when he stayed with Ned, but he asked his hostess for directions anyway. Then she reminded him that the tea shop was open for lunch.

He thanked her, but he didn't have any appetite. Now that he was here, he realized how much he'd lost.

She followed him to the door, pointed him in the right direction, said again how sorry she was, and he was out the door and standing alone on the sidewalk.

He was a little early still, so he decided to walk; besides, if he remembered correctly, there wasn't a big parking lot at the church. He started toward the south end of town. All two blocks of it. For the first few stores, everything looked normal and fairly prosperous. But the sidewalk came to an abrupt end in front of a vacant lot, where weeds grew knee high and had turned brown and brittle. He could see the edge of a couple of discarded tires and what looked like an old icebox lying on its side.

He walked on past two abandoned buildings, which he vaguely remembered as being stores. They were boarded over; the first had lost its steps, and the door stood several feet above the ground. The sidewalk, if there had ever been one, was gone.

He didn't understand how one end of town could have revived and the other been left to die. He willed himself not to look across the street to where the carousel building stood. If it was still standing. There had been near misses during several hurricanes that Cab could remember. He knew there had been more that he didn't know about . . . because he hadn't bothered to take the time to ask.

He suddenly felt uncomfortably hot in his suit and was tempted to take off his jacket until he got to the church. But before he could act, he came to Hadley's, and a smile tugged at his mouth. The single red gas pump, that had been ancient when Cab was a boy, was still standing in the middle of a concrete slab in front of the old clapboard general store, which had once been whitewashed but now had weathered to a dull gray.

Cab took a step closer, stood at the bottom of the steps that led to the sagging porch as if he expected Ned or Hadley to come out the door.

The door opened and a man did come out. He stopped, gawking as if he'd seen a ghost. He was a little softer, maybe a tiny bit stooped. Fifteen years ago, his hair had already receded several inches.

"Makes you look like a MoonPie, only white," Ned would tell him.

"That's not a very nice thing to say," Cab had said. He must have been about eight at the time, on his first trip to spend the summer with his uncle.

Hadley bent over to show his beginning pate to Cab. "You just remember this, young Cabot. 'Cause one day my forehead's gonna push my hair right off my head. And I'll be an egg instead of a MoonPie."

His forehead had been victorious—Hadley was bald as an egg. A rush of affection rolled through Cab. A couple of silly grown-ups, trying to make a lonely little boy laugh.

Cab smiled tentatively.

Hadley squinted at him, then his eyes widened.
"Cabot Reynolds. Is that you, boy?"

"Yes, sir," Cab said, reverting to his childhood
manners—gentleman manners in these parts. And
today they sat comfortably on Cab's shoulders.

Hadley lumbered down the steps and pumped
Cab's hand, then pulled him forward and clapped
him on the back.

"Glad you could make it."

Cab started to say he hadn't known. It was just by
luck that he'd found out about the funeral at all. But
that seemed an indictment of his relationship with
his future wife and a larger indictment of himself.

"You going on over to the church now?"

"Thought I'd walk."

"Mind some company?"

"I would appreciate it," Cab said. Hadley was
wearing a suit, shiny where it had been hand ironed,
and a yellowed button shirt not buttoned at the neck.
As they started down the street, he pulled a paisley
tie out of his pocket and flapped it in the air before
hanging it around his neck.

While they walked, Hadley ran the tie under his
collar, wrapped it, knotted it, and yanked on it until
it turned into a colorful, if somewhat wrinkled, nod
to fashion.

More than ever, Cab was tempted to take off his
jacket. He was beginning to sweat. Partially from

the afternoon September sun and anticipation, and nerves—and a soul-clinging sadness.

They walked side by side in silence. After the initial recognition and hellos, there seemed to be nothing to say. All of their mutual experiences were behind them. The man who had connected Cab to this place was gone. And he felt like an interloper.

The feeling didn't change when, two blocks later, they turned the corner, and Cab saw the Zion Baptist Church a block away. It was a small church, white, with a stumpy little bell tower that Cab didn't remember ever pealing. But it was the crowd out front that checked his steps.

"Got a nice turnout," Hadley said.

"Yeah," Cab said, and cleared his throat. There had to be a hundred people, all ages and colors. Some wore traditional funeral black, others wore a spectacle of bright colors. All the women and some of the men wore hats. All the men wore suits.

As Cab and Hadley approached, the buzz of quiet voices quickened then died as the mourners turned as one to watch them walk the last half block to the church.

Then a man stepped out of the crowd, and Cab recognized the tall, gangly form of Beau Crispin. An old man now, with thick white hair, wearing a dark suit and looking about as uncomfortable in it as Cab felt in his.

He walked slowly toward them, but then Beau

had never seemed to hurry in the whole time Cab had known him.

Hadley stopped, and they waited for Beau to reach them.

It seemed an eon until Beau stuck out his hand. "Knew you'd want to be here. Everybody's real thankful you saw fit to come."

Cab didn't even try to explain why he'd almost missed the funeral. He was still having a hard time understanding why Bailey had kept the news from him. Which was a bit of a lie; he knew exactly why she hadn't told him.

The three of them turned toward the church. "Thought maybe you'd bring that pretty lady you're goin' to marry," Beau said.

Cab jerked his head toward the older man. "Bailey?"

"There more than one?" Beau smiled.

Hadley guffawed.

"No, of course not. It's just—I didn't realize anyone knew that I was getting married."

"Aw, Ned kept tabs on you," Beau said. "Real proud of you and all those fine buildings you've designed."

"Sure did," Hadley said. "Showed that picture of your girl from the newspaper around so much, nearly wore it plumb away."

"The newspaper?"

Hadley and Beau shook their heads at each other.

"Society page," Beau said.

Cab put one foot in front of the other though all he wanted was to run. Start over. Turn the clock back, make better choices, spend more time with Ned. And then he forgot about everything as the crowd surrounded him, shaking his hand, shaking their heads, murmuring condolences, treating him like one of their own .

"I TOLD YOU," Sarah Davis said, squeezing to the front of the crowd and pulling Penny and Bethanne with her. "I'm thinking that suit had to put him back a few hundred."

"Hush," Bethanne said in her ear. "How can you think about money at a time like this?"

"Easy. Ned Reynolds is dead, and I got about twenty kids who aren't . . . yet."

"What happened to 'I don't need no handouts.'"

"This wouldn't be a handout. More like a legacy from Ned Reynolds."

Penny snorted. "Well, at least wait until after the obsequies."

"Why Lord, ain't you fancy with your obsequies," Sarah said, lapsing into an over-the-top Southern accent that she used on various occasions and for various reasons. At the moment, she was just trying to make herself feel better. She wasn't kidding about the children's not being dead yet. Half of them went to bed hungry, at least a few were beaten before they went to bed hungry. And most were so tired after coming home after school and doing chores, they fell asleep over their homework if they even got around to opening a book; all were quickly falling far behind in school, with no hope of catching up.

And it was only September. But it had been happening every year since Sarah could remember. If it hadn't been for Ervina, she would have grown up just like them. But her great-grandmother, for all her crazy ways, knew the value of a solid education and made sure Sarah didn't shirk her schoolwork.

It had paid off, with a grant from Columbia. Bake sales and car washes and the generosity of her poor friends and neighbors had done the rest. Now it was payback time. She was glad to do it, but not in the way they needed. She knew she could make a difference, but she also knew her limits. She was better doing research, being an activist, than she was reciting times tables and trying to get little cutout people and paper trees into a shoebox.

But she was here. The community center's last "director" had flown the coop, taking whatever he could carry with him. The kids had run wild all spring and part of summer.

And Sarah had driven unsuspecting into town for a visit. The mayor pounced; there was no one else. It wasn't something she wanted to do. Sarah didn't say that. She said yes.

Conversation stopped again, and they all looked

toward the street, where a white hearse was rounding the corner. The men took off their hats. Families drew closer.

"Where is Ervina?" Bethanne whispered. "Is she coming?"

Sarah rolled her eyes. "She'll be here. And, I'm sure, in full regalia."

The hearse stopped in front of the church. The door to the church opened, and the preacher, dressed in a black robe, stepped out to welcome the body of Ned Reynolds. Next to him, an old woman swathed in the colors of the rainbow nodded slowly as if hearing the tune of a silent dirge.

From inside the church, the organ began to play . . . at the same tempo as Ervina's nodding head.

The three women exchanged looks.

"You have to admit. She's got some kind of sense," Penny said.

"I try not to," Sara said, and watched as Hadley and Beau stepped away from Cabot Reynolds and joined four younger men, who took the casket as it slid out of the back of the hearse. The crowd parted as they carried it up the steps of the church.

"I think somebody better goose 'The Third,'" Sarah said.

"Why is he just standing there?" Penny asked.

"Probably blinded by Ervina's Sunday go-to-meetin' clothes."

"There. Silas is taking care of him."

A small black man with grizzled gray hair had appeared by the nephew. "Come along now, young Cabot. We goin' inside now." He took Cabot Reynolds's arm and led him unresisting into the church.

The preacher walked behind them. Ervina started to moan.

Chapter 4

CAB NEARLY JUMPED OUT OF his skin when he stepped into the church, and someone behind him moaned. Maybe that old woman standing on the steps like she was sent from some higher being.

Before he had taken two more steps, more moaning joined hers, and by the time he was half way down the aisle, there was a full-blown moaning entering the church.

And then he heard it, slowly morphing out of the hum of voices, a melodic line, growing and wrapping around itself until Cab swore words were being formed. And Cab knew the service had started.

Someone guided him into the front pew. He sat down, looked at the casket, white and shiny. Surrounded by every kind of flower he could imagine. He recognized Bailey's contribution. White, tasteful, but tall and big enough to try to cast a pall over the riot of color that surrounded it. There were store-bought bouquets, florist arrangements, and handpicked meadow flowers already beginning to wilt. The image burned itself on Cab's mind. Each of those flowers seemed to stand out and demand to be acknowledged. They had been given by Ned's friends and neighbors, people who loved him.

The preacher climbed to the pulpit, and Cab slipped on his sunglasses just as someone yelled "Praise the Lord."

Cab hardly knew what happened during the next hour, except that there was dramatic preaching, and amening and singing and swaying, and a gospel choir with organ and tambourines that almost made him forget he was at a funeral.

Then the pallbearers stood and went to stand by the casket. Cab wondered if they expected him to walk behind them since he was the only family member present. Everyone around him stood as the casket was lifted and carried down the aisle. The pastor stopped at the front pew, gestured for Cab to accompany the casket, and he did. He caught sight of Beau Crispin, wiping his eyes with a big white handkerchief, and Cab felt a tear slide down his own cheek.

A little old lady dressed in black sat primly next to Beau. Beau's sister Millie. And next to her a larger woman with crazy white curls framing her face. Beyond them there was a sea of faces. Some swaying and humming, some standing stoically watching. A few reached out to touch the casket in a final good-bye. Silas sat across the aisle a few rows back. His head was thrown back, and he was rocking forward and back. His tears flowed freely. And he wasn't alone.

But it wasn't over, as Cab soon learned. They merely walked around to the side of the church to the cemetery. There was a struggle to get the coffin on the mechanism that would lower it into the grave. There was more preaching and "amening" and swaying.

Someone began to clap. It jolted Cab down to his raw feelings. But it was a slower, rhythmic clap, not applause, soon joined by other hands, and the singing started again, this time an old spiritual that he remembered some of the women who ran the store next to the carousel would sing.

Hadley, Silas, and Beau came to stand with Cab as people filed by and offered their condolences. "So sorry for your loss." "A fine man." "The Lord gonna be happy to have him in heaven." "Amen. He'll make the angels laugh." "He'll be sorely missed." "He's already shining down on us, I can feel it in my bones." "He always had a kind word and a smile." "Amen." "You come on back to the inn. Penny and Bethanne are holding a little reception." "Silas be barbecuing on the beach." "Don't you run off, young Cabot. Everybody's wants to say hello."

"Mr. Reynolds. Forgive me, this isn't the time, but I wanted to introduce myself before you leave. Jonathon Devry. I was your uncle's attorney, and I have a copy of the will if you have time to meet with me before you leave."

"He ain't leaving so fast."

Cab looked sharply behind him; no one was there. Only that old woman who had stood at the church moaning. But she was walking away, head down, supported by a petite young woman with short hair and a black pantsuit.

"Don't mind Ervina," the lawyer said. "She's always making pronouncements of one kind or another. She's sort of a local figure."

Ervina. Cabot remembered her, or not her, but hearing about her. Ervina had the *sight,* could heal what ailed you, could put the hex on you if you crossed her. But she looked like a harmless old woman to Cab. Barely strong enough to hold up the wealth of colorful fabric that nearly buried her in its folds.

He told Devry that he would be leaving that night or early the next morning, he was in the middle of a project. The lawyer understood and offered to take him over to his office. It wouldn't take but a minute. His office was right around the corner, and Cabot would be able to make the send-off before people left.

Cab wouldn't mind missing the send-off. He felt exhausted and out of place. And yet, he wasn't really in any hurry to face Bailey.

It only took a minute. Cab was the sole beneficiary of his uncle's estate, which consisted of a small, tin-roofed cottage, a carousel located at the center of Stargazey Point, a few thousand dollars of savings, and all his other worldly possessions.

Cab thanked the lawyer. Took his copy of the will and the keys to the house and carousel and walked out into the sunshine. He stopped on the street to take off his jacket. He'd put it back on before he got to the Inn. But instead of turning toward the hotel, he crossed the street and walked down a narrow street to where Ned had lived and Cab had spent his summers.

The place was a wreck. It had always been small, a cross between a bungalow and a shack, typical of this end of town. The tin roof looked rusty and probably leaked. The porch sagged. And it was sorely in need of a good whitewashing.

Cab hesitated as he ran the keys through his fingers. Did he really want to go inside and see what state the house was in? He'd sell it, but it was probably unusable except as a tear-down for some greedy developer.

Of course, those greedy developers had been partially responsible for Cab's burgeoning career. He turned to look down the street. The neighborhood was quiet; probably everybody was at the Inn, feting his uncle while he stood here alone.

And he was being rude not to join them. He turned his back on the house and headed toward Main Street, but he knew without a doubt that he'd just left a piece of himself still standing there on the sidewalk. And he knew just as well, he wouldn't be leaving town tonight. Possibly not even tomorrow.

The reception was a civilized affair, especially after the energetic funeral. There were a lot of people missing, and they probably wouldn't come. If Cab had learned anything about loyalty in his summers here, he knew they'd be down on the beach, firing up a bonfire. Bringing out booze and food with equal abandon, planning to celebrate into the night, giving Ned a good send-off, making sure he went and didn't hover around, no longer of this world but not yet welcomed into the next.

Cab wondered if he would be welcome at that celebration.

There were a few local officials waiting in the Inn's parlor to say hello, along with other people he didn't recognize but who remembered him as a boy. Ervina wasn't there, but the young woman who had been with her was. She was introduced as Sarah Davis, Ervina's great-granddaughter and a Columbia University professor on sabbatical to study the Gullah community.

"Can't get her to give up her Yankee ways and move back here where she'd be real appreciated," said the mayor.

Sarah smiled slightly, wryly, Cab thought, before the mayor excused himself to talk to someone else.

Sarah looked at him appraisingly. "He only wants me around to run the community center and keep Ervina from putting the hoodoo on him for talking Silas into selling his barbecue place." She narrowed her eyes at him. "If I believed in hoodoo, I'd have encouraged her to go ahead. Anybody with half a brain would have known Silas's granddaughter could get a scholarship just about anywhere without him losing his property." She gave him an even harder look. "Wouldn't you agree?"

Cab hesitated. Was this little sprite of a Columbia professor baiting him? Now that he'd learned she lived in Manhattan, he began to understand the air of sophistication that stuck out among the rest of the inhabitants even though he sensed she downplayed it quite a bit.

"Cat got yo' tongue?" she asked in a broad, Southern accent, almost as if she had read his mind and was laughing at him.

When she flashed him a wide grin, he knew she was laughing. And if she was Ervina's great-granddaughter, she might just have read his mind.

"So why didn't you bring your fi-an-cey." She drew out the word, and it pissed him off. Where did she get off making judgments about Bailey or him, and it was clear she was making a judgment.

"She had other commitments."

"Uh-huh." Sarah stretched her hand out and studied her nails, which Cab could see were cut short and broken, as if she'd been doing manual labor. Her meaning was clear. And she was pretty much right. Still, Cab didn't need a stranger pointing it out to him.

"So how long you staying, Mr. Reynolds?"

"A day or two. And call me Cab; I'm sure you've called me just about everything else in the book."

Her polite smile turned into a full-wattage grin, and Cab found himself smiling back.

"Touché . . . Cab," she said, dropping the drawl and speaking like a no-nonsense New Yorker. "We'll have to chat more before you go."

Cab watched her walk away, wondering what on earth they could possibly have to chat about.

Just about everyone was gone by six, and Bethanne began cleaning up.

The caterer put a plate of food on the table. "You have to be starving," she told Cab. "You didn't have a thing since you've been here. They'll feed you plenty down on the beach later, but we don't want you passing out from hunger before then."

Bethanne introduced her as Penny Farlowe, owner

of Flora's Tea Shoppe. She was a pretty, middle-aged woman with reddish hair and a weird shade of blue-green eyes.

"And before you ask," Penny said, "Flora's been dead for decades. I inherited the name when I bought the tea shop, so I decided to keep it. Has a certain old-fashioned ring to it."

Bethanne came back with a glass of sweet iced tea. "I thought you might rather have something stronger. But eat first."

"This is fine," Cab said. "Thank you both."

Since they both seemed inclined to stand over him while he ate, he asked a question. "What's with Sarah, the woman from New York?"

He could swear a look of amusement passed between the two women. "I'm only asking because she said she wanted to talk about something." He was pretty sure she hadn't been hitting on him and that she had a very different agenda.

They both shrugged.

"We'll just get on about our business and let you enjoy your food. Holler if you need anything." Penny hustled Bethanne away from the table and out of the room.

The food was too delicious for Cab to pay much attention to his suspicions about Sarah. If she was after money, she was in for a big surprise. Did she actually think Ned had left him a fortune? And if she thought Cab was rich, she'd be wrong about that, too. Cab wasn't poor, but his stock portfolio had taken a hit in the recession, just as a lot of people's had.

Whatever, he'd make a small donation, then be sure to avoid her for the rest of the time he was in town.

Chapter 5

CAB WENT UPSTAIRS TO CHANGE, but when he got to his room, the whole situation poured in on him, and he just stood in the middle of the floral room, stuck. He needed to look at the state of the carousel and figure out what to do with it. He also needed to deal with Ned's house. He'd seen a little real-estate office in the next block. He'd let them have the listing for the house. But the carousel?

Already it was beckoning him. The keys felt hot in his hand, which was stupid. His hands were hot, not the keys. Maybe he was coming down with something. He was feeling a little off-kilter. In a fog. Maybe it was the flu.

Or maybe it was just hard to think with all this floral material and flouncy pillows around. He was a minimalist, a modernist, a steel-and-glass kind of guy.

He pushed open a window, and a breeze wafted in. The sun was going down, and the air was cooling off. He'd go down to the beach. He could hear laughing and talking in the distance; the festivities were continuing. It sounded like an enthusiastic send-off. It would be polite to make an appearance. He'd been invited. Besides, maybe Silas or Hadley or Beau would be down there and give him some advice.

He changed into khakis and a T-shirt Grabbed a sweatshirt that he'd thrown in his suitcase at the last minute and tied it around his neck. No one was downstairs. He put his room key in his pocket and went outside.

The air was bracing, moist, and smelled like the sea. He hadn't noticed that earlier in the afternoon. Too preoccupied. Now it hit him full force, and a sense of déjà vu came over him as he walked across the cracked tarmac and stepped from the Technicolor quaintness into gray abandonment. It was like someone had taken a pencil to the town and tried to erase everything below the line.

He saw the carousel before he wanted to. He'd known that Ned had decided not to reopen it after one of the big storms about ten years before. But Cab hadn't really believed that he could just let it sit idle.

The Stargazey Carousel had been Ned's dream. His avocation. His passion. It wasn't like Ned to give up. But then it wasn't—hadn't been—like Cab to ignore the only man who had loved him unconditionally.

He kept walking, afraid to look closer. He knew what he would find. Rot, mold, termites, structural damage. It was amazing that the old building was still standing. And the animals? They'd withstood three-quarters of a century, and now they were probably unsalvageable.

He passed the octagonal building that housed the carousel. Next to it, an old white cottage that had been a store that sold local crafts was in pretty much the same shape. Only a sign, picked out in blue on a piece of whitewashed plywood, said that it was the community center.

No wonder Sarah Davis walked around with a chip on her shoulder. She probably hadn't bargained for this when she'd taken a year off from Columbia and life in New York City.

The bonfire had been lit, and fireflies of burning embers lifted in the air, only to be snuffed out before hitting the sand. Cab continued to the pier—or at least where the pier had been. Where once the lights of the arcades had led to the dance pavilion at the far end, there was now a broken length of matchsticks, barely standing and off-limits to everyone.

Cab let out a long breath. Pretty damn depressing. No wonder Ned hadn't bothered to reopen. Not even Cab could have helped him with this. Still, he walked through the opening of the seawall, past the rotting pylons that stuck up like ruins from the sand.

He looked to his right, and there, where he always sat, was Beau Crispin, carving at a hand-size block of wood.

He looked up, saw Cab, and nodded.

Cab felt about ten years old again. Standing around waiting for Beau to notice him and nod for him to come sit a spell.

"Wondered if you'd be coming down tonight," Beau said.

"It's a lot to take in."

"Big changes. Kind of a one-two punch if you know what I mean."

Cab waited for clarification.

"Get hit with the big one, and before you can think what you should do, it hits you again, and you have no choice but to fall down."

"Is that what happened to the pier?"

"Pretty much. All those storms, beaches got eroded—hardly any left—we're a bit better down on the Point, but not by much." Beau sliced a curve in the block of wood, blew the shavings away.

Cab didn't bother to ask what he was carving. Beau never told, and he never showed anyone the finished work. It was a weird thing to do, but it was Beau, and everyone accepted him the way he was, a kind, gentle soul.

"How's Miz Millie?"

Beau considered, his knife poised in the air. "'Bout the same. She has her flights, like always. But my other sister, Marnie's, back. She keeps us on the straight and narrow."

"I don't think I ever met her."

"No. She left when she was fifteen or sixteen, must have been. Only came back a few years ago. Guess everyone gets a hankering for home sooner or later."

Cab stared out past the bonfire to the dark sea. It seemed to him that the dusk had been snuffed out instantaneously while he'd been watching Beau. But in its place, high above them, millions of stars winked out of the darkness. Stargazey Point. He'd forgotten. "So are you still living out at the Point?"

"Uh-huh. Good Lord knows the place is falling down around our ears, and I had to sell off some acreage. Taxes have gotten so high cause of the new resorts popping up everywhere, that . . . " Beau trailed off. Blew off more shavings and considered his carving. Cab couldn't begin to guess what it would turn into. It looked like a bulb with a knot on top and some crevices down the length.

"It must have brought in a good price."

"Well about that . . . it could've if I had sold them a piece of beach with it, but I didn't. They took it anyway. 'Spect they're waitin' for me to die, so they can deal with the heirs. 'Course, they'll have to wait for Millie and Marnie to go, too."

He stopped, frowned out into the darkness. "But we'll cross that bridge when we come to it."

"Is that what happened to Silas? Sarah Davis, the woman who runs the community center, said Silas sold out. To send his niece to college?"

"Uh-huh. Then the girl goes off and gets herself a scholarship."

"What are they building there?"

"Nothin'. They only got to the tearing-down stage, then ran out o' money. Should've thought about that before they began. But they'll be back, like hyenas, those developers. Won't be satisfied until they've gobbled up the whole coast."

Cab thought about the closed-community project in the planning stages for Myrtle Beach. He hadn't been to the site yet. The surveyors had made detailed maps of the area. Of course, on paper, there were no existing houses or buildings, just a flat surface on which to draw.

"You see Jonathon Devry yet?"

"Yes. Ned left me everything."

"Don't 'spect there was much to leave."

"No. but I didn't expect it. I'm just . . . I wish . . ."

"I understand, son. And so did Ned. Don't let yourself get all bothered by it. Just know that Ned was real proud of you."

There was a shift in the singing. Several people danced up the beach toward Cab and Beau. They pulled Cab onto his feet and into the crowd.

Someone handed him a beer, someone else handed him a plate of food. When he looked back at the seawall, Beau was gone, but Cab could make out the silhouette of a tall, lanky figure walking down the beach toward home.

Cab was stuffed with good food, slightly drunk, and dead on his feet by the time Silas, Hadley, and several other people whose names he'd learned but was already forgetting, walked him back to the Inn.

He half expected to be locked out since it was late, and he appeared to be the only guest. But the front door opened, the lights were turned low, and a note on the registration desk asked him to turn off the light switch at the top of the stairs.

He staggered up the stairs, turned off the light, and had barely gotten out of his clothes before he fell into bed and into a deep, heavy sleep.

HE WOKE UP three hours later, wide-awake and stone-cold sober. It was still black as pitch outside, so he lay looking at nothing, waiting for sleep to return.

It didn't.

After a half hour, he sat up. Looked out the window. Still dark, only the hush shush of the waves through the open sash. He sat up. He knew what had awakened him. It was a dream. A dream he'd often had as a boy away at boarding school, or at home for the holidays. Riding across the sands on

Midnight Lady's back. Free and wild. And happy.

He turned on the bedside lamp. After three o'clock. Still hours before first light, And longer before he could cadge a cup of coffee somewhere.

He got dressed in the same clothes he'd worn at the beach. He pulled the sweatshirt over his head, and, praying that Bethanne didn't mistake him for a burglar and shoot him into the next century, he carried his shoes downstairs.

The street was deserted—not even a streetlight burned in the darkness. He cautiously made his way to his SUV across the street. Opened the hatch and took out a flashlight. Something scuttled across the sidewalk and into the shadows. It could have been a cat or a rat. He closed the hatch.

With the light bouncing ahead of him, he went straight to the carousel building. Walked around the side, guided by that one small circle of light. Shined it on the padlock that kept the double plywood doors together.

Cab expected the lock to be rusty, so he was surprised that it actually opened on the first try. The door was a different matter. It sagged on its hinges, and he had to put down the flashlight and pull with both hands and all his body weight before it screeched open, leaving a scar on the hard-packed dirt.

He stepped inside but stopped just within the doorway, sure that he'd heard something, a remnant of music, but he must have imagined it. He panned the flashlight in an arc, picking out a piece of machinery, catching something that winked briefly, then disappeared. He walked farther inside.

By feel as much as by memory, he made his way to the carousel. Nearly tripped over something lying on the floor. Some kind of tarp. Then nearly ran into a structure that shouldn't have been where it was.

Cab ran the light over it. The old ticket kiosk lay on its side in the middle of the floor. He sidestepped it and walked to where he knew the carousel would be. Shined the light on the pictures that shielded the engine and music maker. And between Cab and the center, a forest of brass poles stood, silent and unmoving, and at the bottom of the poles, waiting, was nothing.

Cab moved the light. Nothing. Moved it again. Nothing. There were no horses, no chariots, none of the other animals that had once traveled its revolutions. They were gone, all of them.

Had Ned had to sell them off one by one, just to live? Is that why he hadn't reopened. Why hadn't he asked Cab for money? He knew Cab's address; Cab sent him a Christmas card every year. Why hadn't Cab thought to ask?

He ran his hand over his gritty eyes and down his face. How had he let this happen? Why had he forgotten to care about Ned? When had he become so self-centered?

"'Bout time you be showing up."

Cab jerked around. "Who's there?" The light of the flashlight caromed around the room. Hit a new figure standing in the doorway. Passed on, came back to stay.

The old woman in the church. Ervina.

She threw her arm over her eyes, and he instinctively lowered the flashlight.

"You don't need that thing to see. Put it out."

Recovering himself, Cab said, "Unlike like you, I can't see in the dark."

The old women cackled. It sent a chill up Cab's neck. "You cain't even see with the light on. That's 'cause you trying to see what ain't there."

"The animals."

"Them, too."

"What else is there?"

She took a step toward him. He raised the flashlight as if it could ward her off. Not that he was afraid of her. She was small and ancient and maybe weighed as much a piece of driftwood.

She averted her face to keep the light from her eyes.

Cab dropped the light to his feet.

"Stop trying to see something that ain't here no more. Too late for that." Her voice had grown quieter but somehow felt magnified by the dark. "Where you been all this time?"

"I—"

"At least you dressed up real nice for the funeral."

Cab squinted into the darkness. Her voice seemed to be coming from a different direction, but he didn't want to risk blinding her again, so he kept the flashlight lowered to the ground. "Do you know what happened to the animals? Did Ned sell them?"

Silence.

"Well?"

"He didn't sell them animals."

Cab jumped. The words were said in his ear. He could feel the breath of her words on his skin. She was a small woman, and his rational self said she must be standing on tiptoe, but in the dark, with her strange voice, it felt as if maybe she had just levitated from the ground.

She moved closer. "Those animals meant the world to him, next to you. He saved them."

"Where are they?

Silence again.

"Where?"

"I'm thinkin' about tellin' you."

"What's to think about?"

"Whether you man enough to have them."

"What? What the hell does that mean?" Exasperated, Cab raised the flashlight.

There was no one there.

Chapter 6

CAB WOKE TO SUNSHINE AND noise from the street. It took a minute for him to remember where he was since his dreams had carried him to some strange places, places he wasn't anxious to visit again.

A hot shower revived him somewhat. He shaved while he deliberated whether to call Frank for an update of the meeting he'd missed. Decided to let it slide. If there had been a problem, one of them would have called. And his voice mail was empty.

Bailey hadn't called, either. He didn't look forward to that reunion. She'd make him earn back her good graces and hot little body. And nicked himself when he realized that those were the first two things he thought about with Bailey, gaining peace and getting sex.

He pushed the thought aside. Funerals were not the time to sell houses or question relationships. Things got all screwed up because of funerals. He just needed to keep his head, take care of business, and get back to Atlanta and work.

He reached into his suitcase and pulled out a pair of jeans. Looked at them. He didn't remember packing them. But he must have, for the ride back probably. He laughed at himself. That crazy old woman last night had got him thinking all sorts of weird things. He pulled them on, found a clean tee shirt. His sweatshirt reeked of smoke, so he put his jacket over his T-shirt and went downstairs to look for coffee.

Bethanne came out of the office as he reached the lobby.

"Good morning." She smiled, and Cab noticed how pretty she was and wondered what made her smile seem so sad. "Would you like some coffee? It will just take a minute to make." She shrugged apologetically. "I wasn't sure what time you'd be getting up."

"No thanks. I need to take care of some things, and I thought I'd just stop by Flora's and get a coffee to go. She is open?"

"Oh, sure, and she can give you a good breakfast, too."

"Great, thanks." He started to leave. Turned back. "Would it be possible to keep my room for another night? There seems to be a lot of . . . stuff to take care of," he finished lamely.

She laughed. "Of course. In case you haven't noticed, I'm not falling over guests." She slapped her hand over her mouth. "There's nothing wrong with the Inn or anything. It's just—"

"No need to explain. I understand. Tourist season is over, and the sidewalks are all rolled up."

She shrugged again and attempted a smile that Cab was afraid would morph into tears.

"Have a nice day," he said hurriedly, and headed for the door.

It was another sunny day, the air was crisp and clean and tinged with salt. He could hear gulls screeching in the distance. So why did he feel like he was standing under a black cloud, with birds of prey circling his head?

Flora's was open. There were a few customers sitting at tables that were covered in blue-checked tablecloths. Half curtains of the same material. What this town needed was a sleek, nouvelle bistro.

No it didn't. This town needed some paint and repairs, a couple of tons of shipped-in sand, and an ad campaign.

"Sit anywhere you want."

Cab quickly searched for her name. Not Flora, not Sarah, Penny. "Thanks, Penny, but I just wanted a coffee to go if that's possible."

"Of course it's possible, but you'll it enjoy it more

if you sit down and drink it with my asparagus, cheese, and ham omelet and home fries."

"No grits?"

"You can have those, too, but I didn't figure you for the grits type."

"You figured right. But I'm a bit in a bind this morning. Are you open for lunch?"

"Sure am. How do you like your coffee?"

CAB WALKED TO the carousel, carrying his coffee and a bag of cheese biscuits that Penny had forced on him. Actually, he was grateful; he was hungry. It must be the sea air. He'd always eaten like a horse during his summer stays with Ned.

He unlocked the carousel door and carried his breakfast inside. There was just enough light filtering through the lattice for him to see his way over to a big workbench, where he set down his breakfast.

There were tools that looked as if they'd been used recently. Had Ned planned to reopen? Where would he have kept the animals if not here? Cab looked into the shadows. It was clammy, dank; it needed a shot of sunshine and life.

He took a sip of coffee, grabbed a hammer and a crowbar, and went back outside. He started with the first piece of lattice. The lattice had originally been secured by hinges and could be hooked open, revealing the carousel. There were no hooks left, and the lattice had been nailed shut. One yank of

the crowbar, and it splintered into several rotten
pieces. Beneath it was plywood; getting it off was
a harder job. It was newer than the lattice and had
been nailed shut over plastic, which he could see
sticking out from behind the edges.

Which was okay by Cab. It meant that maybe
the damp and the salt hadn't completely crept inside
to rust parts and rot wood. Maybe there would be
something left.

He didn't know why it mattered so much, but it
did.

He carefully leaned the plywood against the side
of the octagonal building. It would have to be replaced by the end of the day. He couldn't leave the
inside exposed to weather and looters and God knew
what or who else.

He quit after the third window and carried his
tools back inside. Enough light came through the
opening to cast light through the room. It poured in
over the long workbench, which Cab could now see
had been used recently.

The first thing he did was lift the ticket kiosk
until it was standing upright. Except that the whole
structure leaned precariously on loose joints, a leaning tower of Pisa in bright colors. He wrestled it out
of the center of the room and propped it against the
wall.

Then he took the flashlight over to the carousel. In the daylight, he could see that the poles were

rusted. The rounding panels, which had hidden the engine and music maker, were gone, and they were covered with a tarp and more plastic sheeting. Not much chance of getting either running again. Not that anybody would want to.

Cab looked up; all the ornamentation was gone, and he could look straight into the gears and rods that drove the animals. Like a strange abstract design with no purpose.

He stepped gingerly onto the platform, tested its strength. Here, at least, the boards had been sealed. Still, he walked carefully in a full circle, making sure the frame was solid. Occasionally, he would hit a pole as he passed by, and it would sway a few times before finally settling back in place.

When he'd made a full circuit, he stopped in front of the tarp that covered the engine housing. It was tied tight, battened down sailor fashion. Beau's work, probably.

It wouldn't hurt to take a look. He untied the tarp and threw it to the side. The engine was still there though the red paint had turned to rust brown, the lettering that spelled out the company logo had faded and flaked away, and Cab couldn't remember who had made it.

It looked like it might work if he'd had a power source, but it wouldn't for long; he could see the beginnings of rust on the bolts and cogs. He jumped back to the platform, went over to search the workbench, and found screwdrivers, pliers, and wrenches lined up across the front. Clean rags, slightly damp from the humidity, were stacked neatly in a cabinet beneath, and in the next cabinet, several cans of WD-40. *The secret to a happy carousel is to keep her oiled and speak sweet to her.*

Ned had taken him through every joint, and juncture, each bolt and spring. The process came back to him as if it had been last summer, not twenty-five summers ago.

Twenty-five.

Cab slowly became oblivious to everything around him except the engine and its parts. There was a breeze off the ocean, but no cooling draft reached Cab down in the housing, and sweat soaked his T-shirt and ran down his jaw to drip off his chin.

He forgot that he was working on a defunct engine, one that probably hadn't worked in years. It didn't matter. It was something he wanted to do. Even if it was a case of too little too late.

He stood, rubbed the small of his back. Wiped the sweat off his face with one of the rags that wasn't covered in oil.

"Thought I might find you here."

"Hi, Beau. I was just seeing if anything is salvageable."

"Oughta be. Ned and I came down here nearly every week, just to keep things primed and ready. In case anybody ever wanted to open up the carousel again."

Cab climbed out of the housing. "Do you think anyone would be interested? I have to say, things are looking pretty bleak around here."

"Well, things have been bad, no use mincin' words about that. But we're slowly but surely coming back." Beau put a greasy paper bag and two Cokes on the worktable. "Thought you might be hungry. I was down at the Tackle Shack and thought you might like a catfish sandwich."

"I haven't had catfish, in . . ."

"Probably since the last time you were here."

"Probably, but it's welcome." Cab finished wiping his hands and tossed the rag aside before opening the paper bag. "Thanks."

Beau twisted the cap off one of the Cokes and handed it to Cab, an action so natural that Cab thought he must have spent a lot of time here with his uncle.

The bottle was cold, and Cab took a long drink. It was sweet and tingling. Something else he'd forgotten. How much he loved Coke. Now it was always Evian or scotch or that luncheon staple, sweet tea. But Coke, that was a workingman's drink.

He opened the sandwich paper and took a bite.

"So what were you doing climbing around down in the engine?"

Cab wiped his mouth with the miniscule paper

napkin and finished chewing. "Just didn't want it to corrode while it was left unattended."

"Uh-huh." Beau pulled a stool out from under the table and sat.

Cab did the same. "Actually, I couldn't sleep last night and came down to take a look."

"Pretty dark last night. Had to turn off the electricity. Ned was failing, no real reason to keep it turned on."

"Why didn't someone tell me?"

"Ned didn't want it that way. Didn't want to interfere with your life."

Cab slammed the Coke bottle on the table. "I would have come."

Beau gave him a speaking look. And what it said was "Would you?"

Cab wadded up the paper bag and looked around for a trash can. Beau pulled a plastic grocery bag from a stash in one of the cabinets. "Better carry that out with me. Don't want to encourage any critter to come looking for food."

Cab dropped the bag into the plastic one, embarrassed by his outburst.

"It's the way Ned wanted it. Simple as that. No use wondering what if."

Cab groaned. "You sound like crazy Ervina. She showed up while I was here and scared the spit out of me."

Beau chuckled to himself. Shook his head. "That Ervina."

"She said Ned didn't sell the animals. But she wouldn't tell me where they are. I don't mind telling you, she creeped me out. Was she telling the truth or just making up more of her crazy stories?"

Beau tied a knot in the plastic bag and dropped it on the floor by his feet.

"Son, there're only three ways to Ervina. She's either pullin' your leg, tryin' to scare you, or tellin' you the God's own truth."

"You forgot hoodoo nonsense."

"Hoodoo maybe, but you better never let Ervina hear you calling it nonsense. She might be inclined to put the curse on you. Just a little one, mind you, just to put you in your place."

"Turn me into a toad?"

Beau's eyes twinkled; it made him look like a young man instead of somebody at least seventy. "Maybe not somethin' that drastic but somethin' to get your attention."

Cab shook his head. He didn't remember Ervina too well. Hadn't thought about her at all until she started moaning at the funeral. When he'd first come to Stargazey Point, he'd been afraid of running into her. Ned had told him she was harmless, but then threw in the caveat, if you didn't do anything bad.

"She'll do it, too. Don't you doubt it for a minute."

"She said she knew where they were. But she wouldn't tell me until she decided if I was man enough to find them. I shudder to think what she meant by that."

"Now that, she was just trying to put you in your place. Ned was well loved around here. He was generous, and he cared about the town and the people who lived here."

"I know."

"And a lot of them are wondering what kind of man you turned out to be. Ervina wants to be sure you'll do right by him."

"How? What does she want me to do?" And why was it any business of hers or anyone's in this town. He shut the thought down the minute he thought it.

"Only Ervina knows that. But let me just say, if you're gonna sell to the highest bidder, I think it would be best to do it all at once and be done with it."

"Sell?" Of course he had to sell. The carousel building was an eyesore. It would have to be pulled down if they wanted to gentrify this end of town. And Ned's cottage, if the outside was any indication of the inside, probably should be pulled down, too. Or he could just leave them to rot where they stood and let the town deal with it.

But if the animals still existed . . . If they were in decent shape, they could bring in a lot of money. Not that he needed it. He was doing just fine. But sell the horses? The sea horse, or the pig? Not Neptune's chariot. Or Midnight Lady? How could he sell her? He couldn't do it. None of them. He just couldn't do it.

So what the hell was he going to do? Just walk away? Maybe they were already rotted, maybe they didn't even exist. Maybe he wouldn't have to make that decision.

Beau heaved himself off the stool. "You think on it some. You'll figure it out. And if you're still here tomorrow, Millie said to invite you for Sunday lunch. One o'clock like always."

"Thanks, thank her for me. I need to get back to Atlanta, but can I let you know?"

"Sure, just call up to the house before you come, so Marnie will know how many places to set. Beth-anne knows the number."

Beau picked up the bag of trash and went toward the door. Before he left, he turned back to the room. He didn't look at Cab but at the carousel, then around the room, a slight smile on his lips as if he were hearing, seeing something only meant for him.

Chapter 7

CAB FINISHED OILING THE ENGINE, then carefully re-covered it and tied it down, though not nearly as neatly as Beau had done. He put away his tools and went outside to nail the plywood back over the openings.

The sun blinded him at first. And it took a few seconds to realize what all the noise was. It was Saturday in Stargazey Point. People were out, doing whatever they did in a town that was obviously in its death throes.

Cab opened his eyes. A group of kids was playing Wiffle baseball in the widened tarmac in front of the pier. An older boy was pitching to them. It was a lesson in futility. The wind caught almost every pitch and carried it away from the batter.

"This is dumb," the batter said, dropped his bat, and wandered away.

"Hey." Sarah Davis, not much bigger than the kids herself, loped down the sagging steps of the community center and grabbed the bat. The remaining kids stepped out of range. Sarah's face went slack, and she glowered at the kids. "What? If I were inclined to smack you, which I am not, do you think I'd use a plastic bat?"

She held it up, frowned at it, and hit herself on the head with it.

A dozen pair of eyes grew round.

"See?" She shrugged. "I'm going inside for a snack." She turned on her heels, barefoot heels, Cab noticed. She barely made it to the door before the kids broke rank and ran after her, crowding through the door.

Sarah turned to where she could see Cab. "Don't even say it."

"What?"

"That it was a stupid game. I knew that. But you can't have them breaking what windows are left in the buildings. And they aren't interested in learning anything. The high point of their day is snack, which is some god-awful generic brand red dye # 2, 3, 4, 5, juice pack and peanut butter crackers."

She pointed the plastic bat at him. "And don't warn me about peanut allergies. These kids are too poor to have allergies."

Cab grinned. He knew it wasn't funny. He could tell she was frustrated. And he guessed the tiny dynamo had a short fuse. "Guess you're not having a very good day?"

"Got it in one." She pulled the screen door open and went inside, letting it slam behind her.

What on earth had possessed her to take over a kids' program? Or maybe she really was here to take care of Ervina. The old woman was certifiable.

He finished nailing the windows shut and went back inside to get his jacket. It was ridiculous to spend any more time here. It was sad to see the old carousel cease to be, but there wasn't much he could do about it. Maybe he could find a buyer interested in restoring it—if, and it was a pretty big if—he could find the menagerie that went with it.

But even a restorer would want to move it to someplace where it would be appreciated, not leave it languishing in a forgotten town devoid of tourists.

But before he left it for good, he turned one last time, looking over the now-darkened space. And he thought he must look similar to the way Beau had looked when he left. One last memory of the lights, the calliope, the circling horses and sea creatures and a small boy clinging to the pole that ran through Lady's middle and riding like there was no tomorrow.

Now there wouldn't be, not for the carousel.

He shoved the door closed, snapped the padlock, and walked away. He was sad. He'd lost an uncle and childhood memories, but he'd lost something more important than that. He just didn't know what it was.

It was time he got back to Atlanta. Have a day to relax before work on Monday. Maybe Bailey would be over her mood though she hadn't called him. Then again, the phone worked both ways, and he hadn't called her.

He still had a couple of things that needed to be done before he could leave Stargazey Point. He walked across the street, nodded to a couple of people as they passed. Kept one eye out for Ervina, not that he expected to see her out in the daylight. She'd wait until dark, when he was alone, and pop up like a maniacal jack-in-the-box.

But when she did, he'd pin her down on where Ned had left the carousel menagerie. If he really had left them anywhere.

Cab walked away from the center of town, retracing his steps from yesterday. Jingling the ring of keys in his jacket pocket. He wasn't looking forward to this, and the sooner he got it over with, the sooner he could be done with it and leave.

Ned's house was in the middle of the block, wedged between other houses, with pretty much the same look and floor plan. A main room and kitchen and bedroom, and another little room that would be a closet in newer condominiums or an office in older ones. It had been Cab's bedroom each summer.

He walked past a rusted Chevy parked on the street, with its hood up. Two young men with Rasta hair were bent over the engine. It would be a miracle if they ever got it up and running again.

One of them straightened up. "Yo," he said in greeting.

Cab nodded and walked on.

He slowed as he came closer to Ned's house. The house next door had pots of mums on the porch steps, deep orange and gold and yellow. An old woman used to live there, Cab couldn't remember her name. She was probably dead by now.

He stopped at his uncle's house and was surprised by his anticipation, excitement, and a sense of relief. But it was feeling from another time.

Today, he just needed to take a look inside and decide the best way in which to deal with Ned's . . . personal effects. Ignoring the burn in his stomach, probably just hunger, he told himself, he stepped onto the porch, felt the boards sag beneath his feet. The house probably wouldn't even pass inspection if he did try to sell it.

He unlocked the door, reached for the light switch, and was surprised when the light came on. Was surprised even more at the sock in the gut he felt seeing the old couch still covered with a bedspread. But it was the folded newspaper on the seat that really got to him. As if someone had been reading and had just gotten up to get a cup of coffee.

The place was dusty, and he wondered why no one had come to clean it after Ned's death. Heart attack, the death certificate said. Swift, inexorable. He never even made it to a hospital.

Cab came farther into the room, letting his hand touch the back of a chair they had found on the curb one summer, the woodstove that heated the place in winter, which Cab had never even seen lit. The floor was made of wood that had never seen a sander or a coat of polyurethane. It was covered by a big oval rag rug that someone had made by hand.

He went into the kitchen, walked across the faded and cracked roll linoleum, and had the oddest urge to take off his shoes.

Off the kitchen was his little room. The door was closed, and Cab hesitated before he looked inside. He guessed it had been converted to a storage room long ago. Ned would have stopped expecting him to visit.

But he hadn't. The room was just as it was the first day Cab had come to the house. Same twin bed, the mattress sagging between the brass bed frame. Cab remembered telling Ned that it was just like sleeping on the carousel with the brass poles all around.

Cab walked in and sat on the bed. It groaned ominously beneath his weight. But he didn't care. He was just beginning to understand what he'd really lost, and he buried his face in his hands and cried.

AT SIX O'CLOCK, Sarah locked the door of the community center. She didn't know why she bothered. It would be a blessing if someone stole whatever junk they could cart away. There was no equipment, hardly any usable furniture, and the man the county had sent in to run the place had not only absconded with the grant money but taken the only working computer with him.

That's what grants got you. Red tape and charlatans. Maybe she should write an article about *that* instead of "The Demographics of the Disappearing Gullah Culture."

Sarah considered herself a civilized woman. She had a PhD, for criminy's sake. She was a professor. She knew not to cuss south of Baltimore. But she didn't know how to inspire kids to make something out of lives that were going nowhere fast.

That was not a part of her article's premise. But it was a reality that had hit her hard the minute she drove into town. You could talk about demographics, study bar graphs, run statistics, but it didn't do squat when it came to hunger, poverty, and lack of hope. Hell, the lack of the ability to even imagine hope.

And what the hell was she supposed to do about it? Write an article or three that no one would read except the department heads, who already had too much to read and only knew the Carolinas from Charleston and the Outer Banks.

And now she was stuck here. No resources, no participants, no interest. And Ervina was relentless. The scariest part of it was that the old lady wasn't crazy. She had the gift. And she was damned and determined to pass it on to Sarah. Hell, if Sarah had an ounce of sense, she'd turn tail and do a demographics of the Harlem Renaissance from the comfort of her Upper West Side apartment—the Upper West Side apartment that she'd sublet until next summer.

She was in no mood to go to the little hovel of an apartment she'd rented in Stargazey and spend the night feeling homesick and depressed. *God, get a life, girl.* Maybe she'd go over to the inn and hit up Cabot Reynolds III for a donation for the center.

What had she just said about taking grants? She meant government grants. She was looking for a personal donation without strings. She at least wouldn't take the money and run. She could buy some tape recorders, some books. Or hell, maybe he'd fork over enough for a secondhand computer. And then leave town and Sarah to her own devices.

She picked up the pace and was about to cross the street when she saw the empty parking spot. The fancy SUV was gone. The son of a—was gone.

"Dammit!"

A spotted mutt that had been asleep in a nearby doorway scrambled up and disappeared around the side of the building.

"I wasn't talking to you," she yelled after him. She

marched across the street and into the Inn. Smacked the bell on the registration desk.

"Coming," Bethanne said from the office. She came through the door the next minute. "Oh. Sarah. What's wrong?"

"Did that . . . so and so check out already?"

"Mr. Reynolds?"

"What other so and so is registered here?"

Bethanne pursed her lips. "Well, you don't have to rub it in."

"Sorry." Sarah's shoulders slumped. "I was hoping to hit him up for a bereavement grant. Guess I'm too late."

"You were going to try to guilt that poor man into giving you money?"

"Not me, the center. And he isn't poor. That car of his probably cost thirty thou, and the watch, the suit? Trust me, the man's loaded. And with a name like The Third, his family is, too."

"You've been living up there with Yankees too long to make you so jaded. He's nice."

"Uh-huh, blame it on the Yankees."

"And sad. When he came back in this afternoon, I thought maybe he'd been crying."

Sarah snorted. "All the way to the bank."

"Sarah, that's not fair."

"I know. I'm just in a rotten mood. But if he's so broken up, why didn't he ever visit the man? He was family." Sarah winced. She'd visited as little as possible since she'd left for college.

"I think we both need cheering up," Bethanne said. "Why don't I grab a bottle of wine from the bar, and we go down to Flora's for supper? Besides, he didn't check out, just had to drive up to Myrtle Beach. Maybe you can hit him up after he gets back."

IT WAS LATE afternoon by the time Cab drove away from Stargazey Point. He just needed some respite from the Point and the situation there. He'd have a nice dinner in an elegant restaurant and maybe check out the building site before driving back to Stargazey. Where first thing tomorrow morning he'd consult Jonathon Devry on—Damn, it would be Sunday, the lawyer probably wouldn't appreciate being called on his day off. Cab should have met with him today.

He hadn't gone five miles when his phone began pinging. He glanced at it; the call log was filling up. People had been calling him, but he hadn't had service there. Great. He just hoped he still had a job and a fiancée.

He still had a job, but there wasn't even a message from Bailey He'd at least called that one correctly.

He put the phone on speaker and redialed Frank's number. Got the machine. "Sorry, there's no service here. If there's an emergency, call the Stargazey Inn,

Stargazey Point, South Carolina. You'll have to look it up. I don't think they have a Web site."

He listened to the other messages. By the time he finished, he was driving into the outskirts of Myrtle Beach, the site of the firm's next big project.

Cab was the main designer. He'd met the developer who was putting up the bulk of the money, but only in Atlanta. Cab had never even come to see where the development would be built. Maybe it was time he did. He gave the address to the GPS and turned left two blocks later.

Like most beach towns, the money was near the water; the farther away you got, the less beachlike the neighborhoods. And Cab had to admit this one was pretty seedy, crammed with check-cashing joints, liquor stores, dives, bars, and Laundromats. Basically an eyesore. He drove past a residential block; the houses were ramshackle, some were deserted. A few had flower beds, even fewer were attempting a vegetable garden. Some kids played in the front yard of one, two men sat on the porch of another. A girl wearing a bright pink helmet rode her bike down the sidewalk. She turned into one of the driveways, dropped her bike by the side door, and ran inside.

Porch lights came on. Cab could imagine people sitting at a kitchen table, home from work, from school, from looking for a job. Where were these people going to go when their neighborhood was razed? Had they all sold out and were just waiting

for the money before moving on? Did they all have
places to move on to?

At the end of the block was a brick school covered
with graffiti and a playground growing weeds. He
turned right. He passed a decently kept park before
coming into another questionable section. He imagined this all gone, a beautiful, self-sustaining town
replacing it, with an ecofriendly place for people to
live. But not these people.

It would be better. It would clean up the community and boost the local economy. But what were
they going to do with all the residents?

He was relieved when he came back to the main
drag. He didn't want to think about what he'd seen.
Or what their future might hold.

He'd lost his appetite for food, especially food in
the rarefied atmosphere of a four-star hotel. Crazy,
but now that he was here, with so many choices and
amenities, there was only one thing he wanted to
do. He made a U-turn and headed south.

Several blocks later, he turned into the entrance
of the Myrtle Beach Amusement Park. It had gone
through several transformations since he'd come
here as a boy, but he found a place to park and wandered inside. There were a lot of families and even
more couples; most strolled or stopped to buy something, eat something, but Cab only wanted to see
one thing. If it even still existed.

He could hear the music before he actually saw

the old Herschell–Spillman carousel. Then he was standing in front of it as it traveled round in a whirl of colors and lights. It seemed as if it could go on forever, but after a few revolutions, it slowed to a stop, and the riders climbed off. The music kept playing, and a new group of people took their places, children running to pick out a special animal, an older couple in one of the chariots, a younger couple sitting on horses side by side and holding hands. The carousel started up again, slowly, then faster and faster.

It was a heady feeling watching it circle, and Cab felt his stress and sadness melt away. When the carousel stopped again, Cab bought a ticket and climbed on.

Chapter 8

SARAH SAT ACROSS THE RICKETY table from her great-grandmother, picking at a bowl of crayfish stew and listening to a lecture. She guessed it was a lecture. With Ervina, you didn't always know if she was talking to you, at you, or just conjuring in your presence.

Sarah would prefer either of the first two. She was an educated woman, knew intellectually that the *gift* actually had some credence, but only among primitive peoples. She also knew it shouldn't give her the heebie-jeebies. But here she was, sitting with the gooseflesh broken out on her arms, her neck hair standing on end, and half-expecting the crayfish to crawl back in their shells and scuttle away.

"Would you just say what you mean?" Sarah said.

"You forget how to listen, girl, up there with all those folks not like us."

Sarah squelched the impulse to remind her great-grandmother that those folks were Sarah's folks now.

"And don't you give me that look neither."

"Sorry," Sarah said, deciding it was better to apologize than ask what look she was talking about.

"I don't want you takin' no money from that man."

"What man?"

"Ned's boy."

"Cabot, III? Why not? He has it; why shouldn't he share it?"

"Ain't his journey. Ain't yours neither."

Sarah grinned. "Don't you worry none. He's not my type."

"That man ain't ready for real love, and when he is it won't be with you."

"Thank God for that."

Ervina slowly narrowed one eye.

Sarah quickly held up her hand—just in case. "Fine. I'll be nice. I'll leave him alone, but Nana," she said, reverting back to her childhood nickname for the old woman, "I got nothing to work with here. No fans in the summer, no heat for the winter. No supplies, not one piece of working equipment. You know I'd never take anything from some condescending jackass who'd expect us to fall at his feet and let him tell us what to do.

"But The Third doesn't give a—hoot—about this town or the people in it. I figure a onetime "contribution" in Ned Reynolds's memory isn't going to mean anything. He'll be gone, and I can do something to help these kids while I'm here. I'll be gone soon enough, and nobody's out there looking for my replacement."

Ervina spit on the floor.

Okay, Sarah had made her mad. Now she was in for it.

"You know I wouldn't take any money with strings attached, from no one who would put demands on the center. But this guy will be gone by Monday. He'll forget about us before he's gone five miles. Though, to his credit, I think he was genuinely fond of his uncle."

"You tryin' too hard, girl."

"You're kidding, right? How do you think I got through Columbia and landed a professorship there? By being a simperin' Southern belle?"

Ervina chuckled; shook her head. "You leave young Cabot be. You promise me, you hear?"

"Just one little check?"

"Nuff of your sass, girl. You think you know so much; you gonna mess up everything."

"Okay, fine. With my luck, The Third would get it in his head to drive up from Atlanta every Friday just to count the pieces of paper we used during the week. Just because he's The Third."

Ervina shook her head. "You stop listening to here so much." Ervina pointed to her head. "And start listenin' here." She pointed to the hollow below her breast.

"My pancreas?"

"You so smart. Finish your soup."

CAB NEVER MADE it to his fancy dinner, but he did discover what might be the best barbecue on the Carolina coast.

He was feeling satisfied, exhilarated, tired, content, and intent on not worrying about what tomorrow would bring. Because he knew tomorrow would bring him home. Atlanta. He had a life waiting there, and a fiancée anyone would be envious of. A great apartment, friends . . . so why was a part of him so reluctant to leave Stargazey Point?

He had good memories of the place, sure, but they were largely centered around his uncle. There was nothing for him here now. Wouldn't even warrant a visit really.

He was fond of Beau and Hadley. But their lives would go on without giving him a second thought.

He should probably just leave tonight. Except that he'd halfway accepted Beau's invitation to Sunday lunch. And he didn't want it to look like he was sneaking out of town without saying good-bye.

It's not like anyone who mattered will be there.

Bailey had been dead wrong about that. They did

matter, and they mattered even more now that he'd come back.

The streets were dark as he drove back into town. It was fall, and the few tourists they'd had had returned to their everyday lives. The locals had gone home to bed to get ready for church or whatever they did on Sundays.

Flora's was closed and dark; Bethanne had turned off the Inn lights though she'd left the porch light on again. Cab parked in his parking place across from the Inn and trotted up the steps.

A rocking chair creaked just as Cab reached the porch. He turned to see who it was, sitting there in the dark. Part of him instinctively stiffened, his reflexes on the alert, though he didn't really think someone would mug him on the porch of the Stargazey Inn. Then again . . .

"You." The voice sounded sepulchral in the shadows.

A chill crept up Cab's neck, followed quickly by annoyance. Ervina. It had to be; no one else had her flair for the dramatic or could sound like the voice of doom.

He peered into the shadows of the porch. Made out the diminutive figure in the rocking chair. "What about me?"

"First thing tomorrow, you go out Moss Hollow Road."

"Why?"

The rocker squeaked again. "Take the left fork 'til you come to the bottle tree and turn in at that path. You'll see a house. You ask for Abraham."

She rocked forward and pushed to her feet.

"Who is Abraham? Is he real? Or some metaphorical symbol that I don't get?"

"Huh. He's real enough."

Ervina went down the steps to the street and slowly walked away.

"Wait. Moss Hollow Road? How do I get there? What's a bottle tree?"

"Huh."

"You better not be sending me on some wild-goose chase."

He could hear her mumbling to herself.

"Ask for Abraham."

BY EIGHT O'CLOCK the next morning, Cab was drinking a cup of Penny's coffee and driving west out of town. Penny had given him directions to Moss Hollow Road and a Danish.

The pastry sat on the passenger's seat. Cab wasn't hungry. His stomach was churning, but his brain needed the caffeine. He hadn't slept well after Ervina's crazy talk about Abraham. He warred with himself, half-believing, half-hoping there was something that Abraham could make clear and chiding himself for falling victim to her manipulations.

So far, he just saw mudflats and marshland, a

few abandoned fishing shacks. It occurred to him he should have filled the gas tank before he left Stargazey Point. There was not a soul in sight. He wouldn't put it past Ervina to send him to the back of beyond just to teach him a lesson. Though he wasn't clear on what that lesson could possibly be.

When he was a boy, he heard talk about Ervina, but he'd never seen her that he could remember. If he had been a local boy, he might have joined the other boys doing nothing all day but getting into mischief. He might have gone with them to spy on the old woman to see if she really was a voodoo witch.

But Ned kept him busy and working on the carousel. Looking back on it, Cab wondered why he hadn't resented being sent here to work. It was hard, sometimes boring, work, waiting for the crowds to come, playing the calliope music over and over again, summer after summer.

At night, when everyone had gone home and the music was quiet, Ned would bring out the store of soft, dry rags, and they'd rub those animals down until they shone, clean away the smudges left by sticky fingers, the spilled soda, the muddy footprints. It was a long day, and it didn't end with the lights and the music, but Cab fell into bed each night feeling happy.

Ned's lacked all the physical comforts of his father and stepmother's house, the air-conditioning, the television, the mall. It also lacked the coldness. Stargazey Point had bugs and heat and hard work. But it was a magic place. A place where Cab knew he belonged. Where he was wanted. Where Ned welcomed him each year like he'd never left. Stargazey Point was more than a summer vacation. To Cab, it was a haven and home.

Moss Hollow Road was paved, more or less, though the sides had crumbled, and there were places that had worn down to the dirt beneath. The surrounding countryside finally changed to low-lying fields and trees. And Cab began to breathe easier now that he was on firmer ground, at least literally if not figuratively.

He almost missed the fork and had to back the Range Rover up to make the turn. He immediately entered a canopy of old trees, oak maybe. Still no sign of a house of any kind. He put his coffee cup in the console holder, slowed down, and leaned forward, looking for a "bottle" tree.

Half a mile later, the tarmac ran out, and the Rover bumped slowly over a dirt road, flanked by dense trees and undergrowth. Cab began to get that prickly feeling again.

Up ahead, he saw a glint of blue; he slowed even more. It was set back in a cleared place by the road. An old bush about eight feet high, devoid of leaves but covered with bottles. They sheathed the tips of some branches and hung from others. Every one of them was blue, the deep cobalt blue that was used for painting window frames and doors, porch ceilings and anywhere else spirits might enter.

Of course, more of Ervina's hoodoo. Nonetheless, Cab stopped alongside the tree, unrolled the window, and heard the slight singing of the bottles as a breeze wafted over them. It was an eerie sound. He eased the SUV forward until he saw the turnoff.

It was hardly more than a path. The kind of path that might lead to a still, or a meth lab, a perfect place for a man to be shot for trespassing and his body never found. But he didn't really think Ervina would send him to his death. He made the turn.

And was immediately surrounded by scrub brush. He couldn't have turned around it he wanted to, and he didn't relish trying to back out. He would go another half mile, and if he didn't find a house with Abraham in it, he'd figure out how to get out and back to the main road.

You're crazy to trust that old woman. She could be totally off her rocker. And no one but Ervina knew where he was going except for Penny, who gave him directions to Moss Hollow Road. And she didn't know which fork he had taken.

The path narrowed, and he rattled and bounced down the narrow lane, dodging branches and vines, trying to keep the Land Rover's paint unmarred.

It came up out of nowhere, the patch of dirt, the shotgun shack.

And the shotgun.

Cab saw the barrel sticking out of a minute opening of the front door. The door opened wider, and a huge black dog bounded out, teeth showing and growling like a fiend from hell.

Cab shut the car windows.

The dog skidded to a stop, braced on all fours and looking hungry.

"So help me, Ervina, if I get my throat mauled because of your sense of theatre, I'll come back to haunt you."

Someone stepped out on the porch. It was an old man, a really old man. With white hair and a white beard. No flowing robe, just a pair of overalls made for a much larger man. Or maybe the larger man who had worn them before he'd shrunk to this shriveled old skeleton.

The old man started down the two steps of the shack, the shotgun pointed vaguely in the direction of the SUV. It seemed to take forever for him to complete the steps, then he limped slowly across the yard toward Cab. He stopped to say something to the dog, who sat obediently, tongue lolling.

Which didn't mean he wouldn't jump up and attack at the merest provocation.

The old guy finally made it close enough to the car to poke the shotgun in the air several times, which Cab took to mean, roll down his window.

He rolled it down enough to converse.

"What you want?"

"I'm looking for someone named Abraham."

"What you want with him?"

"Ervina sent me."

The old man cocked his head; hard eyes glinted out of dark, ashy skin.

"Are you Abraham?"

"Are you Ned's boy?"

Cab nodded. And waited while those flinty eyes studied his face.

"You're him." He lowered the shotgun. Jerked his head for Cab to get out of the SUV.

"What about your dog?"

"He won't hurt'cha now."

Hardly a comforting promise.

"Come on, now, I don't got all day."

What could he possibly have to do today, or any other day, Cab wondered. But he slowly got out of the car, his eyes flitting from the dog to the shotgun and back again.

Abraham grinned. The man was missing most of his teeth. He was *really* old, and it looked like he lived alone out here in the woods. What a hell of a way to live.

As soon as Cab shut the car door, Abraham turned and began to walk around the side of the house. The dog got up and walked by his side, casting occasional looks over his shoulder to Cab.

Cab followed them, wondering where the hell

Abraham was taking him and what he planned to do with him once he had him there.

Behind the house was some kind of building that was half-covered with kudzu. A quiet hum like swarming bees came from it.

Abraham propped the shotgun against the heap. Pulled a heavy ring of keys out of his overall pockets. Looked back at Cab, then yanked at the vine. It came away with a ripping sound to reveal a corrugated shed with a thick, metal door.

Cab's blood began to race, half with anticipation, half with what could only be called fear.

Abraham unlocked the door. The dog whined and tried to push past him.

Cab was getting a really bad feeling about this. He was sure he could take the old man, but the dog was something else.

"Thaddeus, you go on back to the house now."

The dog stopped pawing at the door but stood his ground.

"Go on now." Abraham nudged the dog with his foot.

The dog slunk away.

Abraham waited until he was at a distance, then looked around like he expected someone to be watching. Cab looked, too. Didn't see a thing.

The old man opened the door, flicked a switch, and lights blinked, then slowly began to glow. He stepped aside and motioned Cab in. Cab didn't move.

No way was he going in there and risk the old man's locking him in for some nefarious purpose that he didn't understand. Damn Ervina. Why hadn't she told him what he was supposed to do here?

"After you."

Abraham grinned at him and stepped inside.

Cab reluctantly followed.

Chapter 9

AT FIRST ALL HE SAW were wooden crates, set side by side, creating a center aisle down the middle of the room. The room was much larger and longer than it had appeared from outside. The light was minimal, and his mind was just beginning to grasp what he might be seeing when all questions were answered. The lights popped to full wattage.

And Cab could see the names printed on the wood. *Sea horse, Jubilee horse, Fourth of July stallion. Lead horse.*

He moved slowly down the center aisle. Touching the crates as he went as if making sure they were real. *Neptune's Gondola. Harry the Pig. Rounding Boards and Drum Panels.*

Cab sucked in his breath. "They're all here?"

"Yessuh."

"But he gave up running the carousel."

"Yessuh. After that last big storm, he just got tired. We got all of the horses up to high ground. But he never took 'em out again. Just crated 'em up and told me to take care of 'em 'til you came for 'em."

Cab passed his hand over his face. *Why? Why hadn't Ned called and asked for help.* "I would have come and helped him get them set back up. He could have called me."

"He could have."

Cab shook his head, walked away from the old man, farther into the building, into the crates that housed Ned's life's work.

Cab was halfway down the aisle before he saw her. Standing at the very end of the aisle between the crates, mane curling wildly, nostrils flared, black as the night. *Midnight Lady.*

Cab's footsteps slowed, stopped altogether. He glanced over at Abraham.

Abraham slowly nodded. "Go on, boy. She been waitin' for you. She been waitin' a long time."

Cab continued on, and, after a few more feet, he realized that Abraham wasn't following. He reached the carousel horse. She was standing on a platform, her body supported by a muslin sling that was connected to two end supports and run under the length of her body.

Slowly, Cab reached out his hand. His fingers stopped an inch away from her shiny surface. He was hesitant to touch her, he didn't know why. Like maybe he didn't deserve to even see her again.

"You're as crazy as Ervina," he said under his breath. He glanced over his shoulder to see if Abraham had heard. But Abraham was walking away. Cab turned back to Lady, his fingers still poised an inch away. "Hi, Lady." His hand gently touched her back.

EVERYTHING HE KNEW about her, every ride he had taken, every dream he'd ever had seemed to rush in on him, the way they said your life passed before your eyes right before you died.

Strange ideas began to swirl in his head. It was the magic of the carousel. Cab had never called it that. At least not since he'd gone off to school, but he'd felt it often as a boy. He'd believed it was real, that magic. But he didn't know where it came from now.

Carousel magic was for children . . . and for his uncle. He smiled. Ned's passion. He'd saved that passion for Cab, when he could have sold it and lived comfortably for the rest of his life.

But that was crazy. What did he expect Cab to do with them? He'd have to sell them, he couldn't subsidize the running of a money-losing carousel in the back of beyond. Is that why Ervina hadn't wanted to tell him where to find them? Because she knew he would have to sell them, at least donate them to someone who could preserve them properly.

Hopefully, he could find one buyer who would not sell them piecemeal to the collectors who had sprung up over the last decade or so. Would he sell Lady, too? He couldn't keep her. It would be sacrilege to have her standing in his living room. Alone, away from her mates.

Maybe he should just leave them in storage. He could beef up the structure. Add better climate control. He could have them moved to a climate-controlled storage unit closer to Atlanta.

He coughed out a laugh. Rested his forehead on Lady's sleek shoulder. What was he thinking? How long would he keep them locked away? Until he retired? Would he then come back to run his uncle's carousel? An old eccentric architect . . .

He reluctantly stepped away, his eyes feasting on Lady's glossy black coat, peered into her wild eye as if she could read his mind. *Good-bye.*

He'd left her many times over the years, but it was worse now because he knew this would be for the last time.

He turned away. He was being crazy. It was a wooden horse. That's all. Just wooden animals. But as he made his way back down the aisle, the crates seemed suddenly alive. Buzzing, as if trying to get his attention, as if they were talking to each other and to him. It had to be the memories, or that crazy Ervina planting things in his head; maybe he was coming down with the flu. He hoped he wasn't losing his mind.

He pushed out into the sunshine, closed the door, locked it. He stood unmoving, breathing hard for a few moments, then walked around to the front of the shack on rubbery knees.

Abraham was sitting on the stoop, his shotgun across his lap and the dog lying at his feet. They both pushed to their feet as Cab reached them.

"Everything seems to be in good shape," Cab said, grasping at normalcy. "I didn't open any of the crates, but if Lady is any indication, then the rest should be good."

"They be good. Got a bit of damage, some of 'em, but Mr. Ned, he worked on 'em, so they wouldn't get worse. They been locked up tight so no weather or critter could get to 'em."

"I don't suppose he told you what I was supposed to do with them?"

"He said you'd know what to do."

"Great." Cab frowned at the old man. "Do you come with them?"

"No suh, I just been sittin' with 'em until you come to get 'em."

Cab rubbed his chin. Christ. He needed to think. Make arrangements. Buy some time. "Would you be willing to, uh, sit with them a while longer? I'd be willing to pay you extra."

"Go on now. This is my home." He lifted the shotgun. "I'll make sure nobody gets near 'em. But don't take too long. Those animals'll last longer than both of us. So don't you take too long."

"No. I'll be in touch." Cab didn't even ask if there was a phone number where he could be reached. He would just call Sarah Davis and have her tell Ervina what he decided. Then Ervina could teleport or telepath, or whatever she claimed to do, the message to Abraham.

Cab drove back to town, thinking about Ned's leaving the animals under Abraham's armed guard. His mind was in turmoil. Bailey had been right after all, but for the wrong reasons. He shouldn't have come—because these people mattered. They mattered more than they should. Would he forget about them once he got back to Atlanta?

Probably. Life would go on, he would get busy, Ned would slip back into that quiet place in his heart and gradually fade from thought. Bethanne, Penny, and Sarah would mesh into vague memories, Beau and Hadley, even Ervina would be pushed to the back of his mind and slowly forgotten.

Is that what he wanted? And how could he explain to them what he felt and what he was going to do?

When he got back to Stargazey, he parked at the Inn, but instead of going inside, he walked down the street to Hadley's store for a cold Coke.

He pulled a bottle out of the ancient cooler on the porch. Let the cold, melted-ice water drip off the bottle onto his fingers, then to the floor. He turned to go inside to pay just as a little boy ran out the door.

"Grab him," Hadley yelled.

Cab scooped the boy up and carried him, kicking and wriggling, back into the store. Cab set him down on the wooden floor but kept a firm hold on his arm. He couldn't be more than five years old, too skinny, and already shoplifting. It was sad.

Hadley came around the counter and frowned down at the boy as he struggled to get away.

"Now what do you have there, Joe?"

Slowly, Joe stretched out his hand to reveal a candy bar.

"Only got one?"

The boy's eyes bugged, and his bottom lip protruded like he might cry. Cab reached for his wallet.

Hadley shook him off. "You gonna share that with your sister?"

Joe was looking at the ground, but his head bobbed up and down.

"Don't you think maybe she might want her own Mars bar?"

The head pumped up and down.

Hadley reached over to the candy display and got another candy bar, which he stuck below Joe's bowed head. Joe looked up, his eyes round and full of disbelief.

"You go get Dani, and you both come eat your candy right here on the porch, where I can see you."

Joe grabbed for the candy, but Hadley held it away and managed to extricate the other one from Joe's hand.

"Hadley," Cab protested.

"You go get her and bring her here. And you'll get your candy back."

Joe bit his lip, then shot toward the door. He was back two minutes later with his body double. "Here she is," Joe panted out.

"Mornin', Miz Dani. Now you both come here."

They walked dutifully toward Hadley, heads lowered. Joe was visibly shaking.

Hadley squatted. "Joe, have I ever laid a hand on you?"

Joe's head wobbled back and forth.

"No one's ever gonna hurt you in this store, you get that?"

Both children nodded in tandem.

"No one." Hadley held out the candy bars.

Dani and Joe just looked at them.

"You know stealing's a crime."

"Don't send us to jail," cried Dani.

"I ain't. I'm gonna give you this candy. But I

better never ever hear or see you do any stealin' here or anyplace again. If you need something that bad, you come and tell Hadley, and we'll see what we can do. Understand?"

Two children nodded.

"Now go out and sit on the porch and eat your candy. And don't tell your uncle nothin' about this."

Both heads shook. Two hands simultaneously reached out and snagged the candy bars. They shot out the door together.

"They don't have nothin'," Hadley said. "'Ceptin a drunk for an uncle, who beats 'em. Crying shame."

"That was a nice thing to do," Cab said, and pulled out a ten for his Coke.

"We all try to look out for them. Don't know why they don't learn to ask for what they need." He handed Cab his change.

"Keep it."

"You don't have to do that."

"I want to. You can order more candy bars for next time."

"Well, I thank you. So Beau said you were over at the carousel yesterday."

"Yeah. It's really a mess."

"Too many storms, too hard to keep up. Ned couldn't find steady workers to help him run the thing."

"Yeah, this end of town seems to have gotten hit worse than the rest."

"Maybe a bit, but this whole town is going to hell in a handbasket, I don't care how many times you paint it." Hadley sighed. "It's hard to keep rebuilding time and again, and after Ned closed down the carousel for the last time, well, folks just kinda let things go."

"You all blame Ned?"

"Hell no. Just saying that things kind of centered around the carousel and the arcade and the beach. They're gone. So are the tourists. Just what happens. 'Course, if somebody decided to reopen the carousel, things might start lookin' up. Give people some inspiration to get up and go."

"You know anybody who wants to take over? And who can afford to take over? I'm not turning those animals over to somebody who won't take care of them."

Hadley's expression changed. His eyes sparked with curiosity. "So it's true. About the animals. Ned did get them to safety. They survived?"

"Well, yeah. They did. Was it a secret?"

"Sure the hell was, and you'd best keep it that way. There's been plenty of talk, but nobody knew if it was really true."

"He didn't tell anyone?"

"Not that I know of. Was afraid it would get out. I guess those animals are worth a lot of money. He didn't want no strangers gettin' their hands on them."

"Well, thanks for the Coke and the talk, Hadley. I better get cleaned up. I've been invited to the Crispins' for Sunday lunch."

"Hope you decide to stay a while. And ask Beau Crispin about those animals. He and Ned were pretty good friends."

"I will, thanks."

Cab returned to the Inn. Bethanne came out of the parlor as soon as he reached the foyer.

"Is it true? Did you find the carousel horses?"

Cab stared at her. "Who told you that?"

Bethanne blushed. "I'm sorry. I didn't mean to jump the gun. But Penny told me. She heard it from someone who came into the tea shop this morning. They said you might be thinking about reopening the carousel. That would be so great. A real boost to the town. Bring in the tourists again and put Stargazey Point back on the map."

Her face fell. "You look surprised. Guess it was just a rumor."

"Afraid so," Cab said. "I'll be leaving in the morning if you would prepare my bill. Now, if you'll excuse me, I have to get upstairs and change." Cab trotted up the stairs. Were these people so desperate they thought he would actually reopen the old carousel? Put in the money it would take to refurbish the existing equipment, sink a bundle into a new engine, music box, and the building—though he wouldn't mind getting his hands on the building.

It was a classic example of early-twentieth-century pavilion-style architecture. But he wouldn't have time to do any restoration work with his current schedule. He wished he did. He'd always loved working with his hands; it was something he missed.

But he wouldn't have the time, and he'd have to trust some local contractor to do it correctly. And hire people to maintain it. And to dismantle it in case of another hurricane. And who the hell could he trust to operate it day after day and give it the same kind of attention and love as his uncle Ned?

Maybe he would leave tonight. Get back to Atlanta, where things were normal—career, wedding, friends. Where his mind didn't question everything he thought or did. Atlanta, where his future was mapped out, solid, safe.

Chapter 10

CAB DELIBERATED ABOUT DRIVING TO Crispin
House. It wasn't that far, but the fall had been dry,
and if he walked, he risked arriving with dust-
covered shoes, which he didn't think Miss Millie,
whom he remembered as slightly eccentric, would
appreciate.

But he had a lot to think about, and the walk
would help clear his head. He dressed in slacks and
shirtsleeves, added a tie at the last minute, and hoped
to hell they hadn't expected him to wear a jacket for
lunch. He'd only brought his funeral suit, and he
had no desire to put it back on anytime soon. He
wore his good shoes. He set out at a quarter to one,
with the shoe buff cloth from his room's amenities
basket in his pocket.

Cab walked down the road and onto the drive

that ran beneath a canopy of moss-dripping trees. It was like stepping back into a time tunnel, he thought, as the sun was blocked out and the air grew chill. Minutes later, it spit him out at the other end of the drive and Crispin House.

Crispin House was a huge, neo-Italianate mansion on the point of land that gave the small town its name. At one time, the Crispin family had owned pretty much all the waterfront property on both sides of the point.

It must have been glorious back in its heyday, but now it would barely pass as shabby-genteel. It was desperately in need of a coat of paint. The porch was dotted with buckets, which, considering they were upended, must denote rotten floorboards. It needed help, and Cab's hands itched to begin repairs.

But it would be totally rude to even mention the sorry state the house had fallen into. Better just to pretend not to notice.

He went up the steps rather cautiously. Rang the ancient bell, listened to it echo hollowly from inside the house. He could almost imagine a black house slave answering the door and was relieved that it turned out to be Beau.

"Come on in, the girls are in the parlor."

The girls? For a second, Cab was at a loss, then realized Beau must be talking about his sisters, Millie and the other one, the one who'd left Stargazey as a teenager. Had Beau mentioned her name?

Beau ushered him through a wide archway into a huge parlor, filled with antiques.

A sofa and love seat faced each other in the middle of the room, with two chairs completing the square. Two women sat facing each other.

"Here's Cabot," Beau announced.

Both women turned toward the door.

Cab recognized Miss Millie immediately. Older, yes, but with that same not-quite-here aura about her, as if she were channeling a Southern belle, or a character from a Tennessee Williams play. She was dainty, with fine white hair pulled back from her face.

But it was the other one that grabbed Cab's attention. She was more like Beau, lanky and tall, slightly rawboned, with a head of wild gray-white curls.

"Why, how you've grown," Millie said, interrupting Cab's inspection of her sister.

"Good to see you again, Miz Millie."

"Oh for crying out loud, Millie, of course he's grown." The other sister stood. "Marnie Crispin." She stuck out a large, callused but somehow feminine hand, and they shook. "Call me Marnie, drop the Miz if you don't mind."

"Sister," Millie admonished.

Marnie smiled at Cab.

"Cab Reynolds."

"Nice to meet you, Cab. I remember your uncle. Nice man as I recall."

"He was," Cab agreed.

"Cabot, you just come sit down by me and tell me all about what you've been doin'. And about that fiancée of yours."

"The third degree," Marnie said under her breath, and sat down again. Cab took a place on the love seat next to Miss Millie.

He told her about his college and his position at Bloomquist and Ryan.

"Ned said you designed big malls and things."

"Yes, as well as other things."

"Like?" asked Marnie.

"Like . . . We'll soon be breaking ground on a huge, self-sustaining community in Myrtle Beach."

"How nice," Millie said.

"One of those places where you never have to leave the compound and mix with the hoi polloi?" Marnie asked.

Cab glanced at Beau, who had sat down in the chair between the sisters and was slowly carving a new, unformed block of wood.

"Pretty much," Cab said. "An efficient, convenient way to live."

"Sounds just god-awful to me," Marnie said, then tempered it with a smile. "But then, I've always been one for freedom."

"Hmmph," Millie said.

Beau continued to carve.

"Now tell me all about your fiancée, what's her

name? Ned must have told me a hundred times. I just don't remember things like I used to."

"Bailey," Cab said.

"That's right, Bailey," Millie said. "Well, I'm sure she's a lovely girl. Do you have a date set for the weddin'?"

"Yes, sometimes in the spring, not this coming spring but the next. I'm leaving all the details to her family."

"Isn't that just like a man? You better write the date down; we wouldn't want you to miss the ceremony, now would we?"

Cab realized that Millie was flirting with him.

Marnie stood. "Never understood these long engagements. I'll just get lunch ready."

"We let the staff have Sundays off," Millie explained.

Beau looked up from his carving, exchanged looks with Cab. It was unnecessary. They didn't have house staff. From what Cab had heard in town, the Crispins were lucky to even be living in the house. They were always behind on their taxes, and the developers were constantly at the door with offers to buy them out.

So far, they hadn't sold outright, and the property hadn't been seized. They'd managed to stay one step ahead of the tax collector by selling off smaller parcels. But according to Hadley, it was just a matter of time.

The house would be a tear-down; that would make the most sense financially. Cab bet it would cost a fortune to bring the old house up to code. But it would be a shame. He could imagine it in its former grandeur. It just needed lots of money and love and time.

Like Ned's carousel.

A few minutes later, Marnie called them into the dining room. Even with the leaves taken out, the table was huge, and the four place settings were clustered around one end. Mille sat at the head, which Cab thought odd since it was usually the head of the house who had that honor.

Lunch was roast chicken with greens, buttermilk biscuits with chicken gravy, and boiled potatoes. Simple Southern fare. Something Cab hadn't eaten in years, he realized. His diet these days consisted of sandwiches at his desk, business lunches of drinks and steaks, or rabbit-food dinners with Bailey.

He had seconds of every dish, which seemed to please Millie and amuse Marnie. Beau was as unruffled as ever.

After a dessert of peach cobbler—"We canned them ourselves," Mille told him—they returned to the parlor.

Cab was beginning to imagine a long, boring afternoon ahead of them, when Beau said. "Thought I might take a look at that railing on the porch roof if Cab wouldn't mind holding the ladder."

"I'd be glad—"

"Don't be absurd, Beau. We just finished lunch," Millie scolded. "And you have no business climbing up that ladder. A man your age. And on a Sunday."

"You gonna do it, Millie?"

"Hush up. You can call over to the center tomorrah and ask Jerome to help you."

"I could, but I got Cab here today. Once we figure out how bad it is, I'll know what to tell Jerome to do."

"I'd love to help, but I'll do the climbing." Cab smiled at Millie, patted his stomach. "I need to keep my figure after that delicious meal."

Millie beamed. Marnie rolled her eyes. Beau said, "It's right out here." And Cab followed him outside.

There was a quick tussle over who was going to climb the ladder, which Cab won. The ladder was old and none too stable, and the second floor was a long way away.

He slung Beau's tool sack over his shoulder and climbed up to the porch roof. He tested the old rail, which wobbled in his hand. It was wooden and made up of posts and panels of geometric pieces that formed a bull's-eye pattern. Half the wood was completely rotten.

Cab looked down at Beau. "I can stabilize the posts for now, but I think you'll have to replace this entire panel, and if there are others this bad, you may have to replace all of them."

He could tell by Beau's expression that it wasn't what he wanted to hear. "I was afraid of that."

Cab pulled out the hammer and a handful of nails and set to work stabilizing the posts. It was a temporary fix. The whole railing needed to be replaced. He had to search for a sturdy section of wood to drive the nails through. He made the railing as safe as possible with his limited tools, then looked down at Beau.

"I think it'll hold for a bit, but don't let anybody go leaning on it. Your best bet is to replace it with wrought iron or even PVC." Cab cringed as he said the latter; the old house deserved better than that. It deserved a meticulous restoration, but plastic would be cheaper and easier to maintain in the long run."

"Thank you, you come on down now."

Cab climbed down and brushed the flakes of paint off his hands. "You've also got some missing shingles on the porch roof."

"I been meaning to get to those."

"I could . . . I can't promise, but I will probably have to come back to finish settling up Ned's estate. I might be able to help you then."

The old man's eyes lit for an instant, with anticipation or hope? And for that split second, Cab remembered him younger, athletic, with blue eyes that twinkled just like Cab imagined Santa's would do.

"'Spect you'll be needing to get back to Atlanta

soon," Beau said, as they carried the ladder to the back of the house.

"I'll probably leave this afternoon. Big project ahead of me."

"Your private town in Myrtle Beach?"

"Yes."

"Don't pay Marnie no mind. She speaks hers as she sees fit."

"Oh, I don't. I appreciate her, um, forthrightness."

"That's one way to describe it." Beau smiled fondly. "She's something else."

"Actually Beau, I could use your advice on something."

"Don't know as I can help, but I'll try."

"I saw the animals."

Beau nodded. He didn't have to ask. He knew what animals Cab was talking about.

"Ervina's known all along. She finally sent me to this old man named Abraham."

Beau nodded again.

"Did you know where they were?"

"No, I didn't. Ned thought somebody besides Ervina should know, in case . . ." Beau hesitated. "If anything happened to her . . . But we both decided that they would be safer if nobody knew. Word gets around here, seems like whether you tell it or not."

"I know what you mean. Bethanne already heard I was reopening the carousel."

Beau chuckled. "People still got hope."

"I have a career, work back in Atlanta. I'm about to get married. Even if I found someone reputable to run the carousel, it would cost a fortune just to restore, and I haven't even looked to see what shape the animals are in."

Beau nodded. "I 'spect it would."

"But I can't see selling them. Not for a while, anyway. That just doesn't seem right, somehow. But I also can't expect Abraham to sit there for God knows how much longer while I decide what to do with them."

They'd come back to the house and climbed the steps to the porch.

"Guess I'll say good-bye to Marnie and Millie and hit the road. Thanks for everything, and especially for calling me. I had no idea Ned had died."

"Didn't think you did. That's why we decided to make sure for ourselves."

"You and Hadley?"

"Me and Hadley and Ervina."

"Ervina?"

"She promised Ned she would take care of things."

"That sounds kind of ominous."

"It can be. But she won't harm you . . . unless you need harmin'."

Cab shuddered even though he knew it was just more of the local mumbo jumbo.

"Now you don't keep worrying. I 'spect you'll figure out what to do."

Cab said good-bye and walked back to town, feeling as unsettled as he had before talking to Beau. He paid for one night since Bethanne refused to let him pay for both, and carried his bags out to the Range Rover.

Bethanne followed him to the sidewalk. "You come back now. You're welcome anytime."

He nodded, but he couldn't speak. He suddenly wanted to see the inside of the carousel and Ned's cottage just one more time. To touch Midnight Lady. But that would be dangerous. Something was shifting inside him. An attachment that had weakened over the years had come back full force this weekend. He didn't trust it. He had to leave it behind, once and for all. A clean break.

He kept his eyes on the road ahead as he drove out of town. He didn't even drive by the cemetery. He wouldn't know what to say to his uncle if he did.

Chapter 11

SARAH WAS SITTING AT FLORA'S Tea Shoppe when she saw the Range Rover drive past. "Now where's he going?"

Penny, who had just sat down for a break after the lunch crowd, craned her neck to see over the blue gingham half curtains. "Not here for lunch, that's for sure."

The phone rang. Penny jumped up. "Please let that be a catering gig."

Two seconds later, she hung up. "That was Bethanne. He just checked out."

"The hell he did." Sarah jumped up. Her coffee cup rattled on the table. She headed out the door.

"You think you can outrun him?" Penny said, following her out to the street. Several doors down, the gate to the inn opened, and Bethanne hurried toward them.

"Why did you let him go? I wanted to hit him up for some cash for the center."

"I couldn't help it. He came back from lunch with the Crispins. He was going to leave tomorrah, but he said he'd miscalculated and had to get back for a meeting in the morning that he didn't want to miss."

"Probably couldn't wait to unload those carousel animals. Some of them have to be worth twenty or thirty thousand apiece."

"No way," Bethanne said.

Sarah nodded. "Not all of them, I seem to remember Ned Reynolds had to replace a few of them after one of the storms. Those I think were fiberglass or something and would be less valuable. But don't quote me."

"That's where he went this morning?" Bethanne said. "He was going to look at the animals?"

"Looks like it. Well, to hell with us, and to hell with him, too."

"Were you really going to ask him for money?" Penny asked.

"Damn straight."

"I don't believe you."

Sarah frowned. "Why?"

"You soliciting, much less asking for money from a rich white guy?"

Sarah broke into a grin. "You know me so well.

Actually, I confess I was having second thoughts about it. He caught me in a weak moment."

"Well, I don't see anything wrong in accepting money for a good cause, no matter the gender or color," Bethanne said tentatively.

"That's why we love you," Penny said. "Come on in, and I'll make us fresh coffee."

The three women turned to go into the tea shop.

Ervina was standing in the doorway.

Bethanne squeaked, Penny froze, Sarah frowned at her great-grandmother. "Damn me, Ervina, why do you do that?"

"Watch what you say, girl. You might get what you wish for."

Even Sarah recoiled at that one. "I didn't mean it. And I don't believe in curses. Though if I did," she added under her breath, "I'd put one on the man driving out of town.

"He already got one on him."

Sarah groaned. "Please tell me you didn't do anything to him."

"Not my doing. He brought that one with him, and he took it back with him. It's riding on alongside him in that big car of his."

"What is she talking about?" Bethanne whispered to Penny.

"Not a clue."

"Did he really find the carousel animals?" Sarah asked.

Ervina nodded.

"What's he going to do with them?"

"Up to him."

Ervina walked past them and started down the street.

"Is he coming back?"

Ervina paused, looked back over her shoulder. "How do I know?" And kept walking.

CAB FELT THE heaviness close in almost as soon as he reached the highway. The weekend was just catching up to him. The drive, the funeral, the carousel, the crazy people, the little town gasping its last breaths. It would be good to get back to the city, where things were set, where he knew where he stood.

He had a good job, a great job. And a fiancée any man would be proud of and who could help his career. A major project that would push him up to the next level.

The girl in the pink bike helmet pedaled across his mind and disappeared.

He shook off the image. The residents in Myrtle Beach would find a better place to live. A nicer neighborhood.

Like Stargazey Point? Is that what you want for Stargazey?

Stargazey was different. It had a history. It could make a comeback.

The Crispins are one step ahead of the tax assessor. Do you want what happened to Silas's barbecue place to happen to them?

"No." But it wouldn't happen to the Crispins.

Who was he kidding? It happened all the time. Up and down the coast, whole villages disappeared, to be replaced by exclusive homes, yacht clubs, and resorts.

By the time he reached the outskirts of Atlanta, his stomach was tied up in knots. His mouth was dry, his eyes hurt. The skyline was rising before him, beautiful, in a remote, aesthetic way. But he didn't feel the same joy he'd felt when he saw the ocean as he drove into Stargazey Point.

But it was always like that when you got back from a vacation. The reluctance to give up the relaxation and get back to the grind.

Only usually, he couldn't wait to get back.

Well, this was different. An obligation. Not a vacation at all.

You've got unfinished business in Stargazey, and you know it.

He would call Jonathon Devry in the morning and tell him to sell everything.

But the troubling feeling followed him through the garage and up the elevator to his condo. He'd called Bailey from the road as soon as he had phone reception and left a message that he was on his way home. He'd called Frank and left him a message saying he was coming back tonight and would be at the meeting tomorrow morning.

He let himself into his apartment, threw his bag on the closet floor, and fixed himself a drink. He was standing at the window looking at the view when Bailey walked in.

Good, back to normal. They'd have a nice nouvelle dinner that didn't include grease, fatback, or carbohydrates, they'd come home and have makeup sex. Tomorrow, he'd work on the Myrtle Beach plans. Get back to work. He had some dynamite new ideas for the project.

He turned, with a smile forming on his lips.

Bailey pushed her glossy hair back and came toward him, leisurely, not rushing, building the anticipation. She dropped her purse on the couch and gave him her pouty look.

And Cab felt one thing. An overwhelming desire to run.

He checked himself, finished his drink, and came to her. Kissed her like he hadn't seen her in months instead of two days. His body responded like it always did, but he felt somehow disengaged.

He was tired; by tomorrow, they'd slip seamlessly back into their lives like nothing had changed.

But something had changed. Cab didn't know what exactly, just that it was going to be major, and he had no idea how to plan to face it.

She took his hand, pulled him toward the bedroom.

"We have to hurry," she said in that soft seductive voice. "Frank, Tony, and George Erickson are meeting us for dinner. George is anxious to get started on the demolition in Myrtle Beach."

Chapter 12

THEY WERE ONLY A FEW minutes late to the upscale fusion restaurant called Vim27. The ever-present chic modern décor, the bleached wood and black metal, recessed lighting, bamboo floor and walls. Red ceramic plates. It reminded Cab of his apartment, clean, sleek, and cool. Cutting-edge in every way. So slick, he felt a chill.

His mind drifted toward Bailey, but he pulled away from his thought before it could take root. He was getting married next year.

George had managed to get a reservation for one of the private rooms, and the five of them sat around the polished table as if they were at a board meeting rather than a social dinner.

Which was probably the case. Cab hadn't missed

the round tubes of plans that Frank carried in and deposited in the corner.

Bailey was laughing with George and Tony, but she'd have a fit when she realized they would be talking business as soon as the dishes were cleared.

Then again, Bailey would do anything to advance his career. Cab looked from her to George to Frank to Tony. And he wondered how far she would go? He shook the thought off. What was wrong with him?

He should have canceled. Told them he was too tired to meet tonight. He felt cold, hot, both. His head hurt. He needed to think. Something was suddenly not right in his life. It would probably pass, but he didn't want to have to make any decisions about buildings or life tonight.

After dinner, the table was wiped by a silent busboy dressed in a print sarong. Frank opened one of the tubes and spread out the plans, using all their cell phones to hold down the corners.

"This is what we worked out on Friday when you were gone. Hope this is in line with what you intended."

Cab glanced at the spec sheet; there were several new squares of various sizes. A small square depicting a guard kiosk sat exactly on the spot where that little girl had left her bike. Where would she ride? Where would two ignored children steal candy and not be punished but shown compassion?

Drugs, drinking, poverty, he reminded himself. Abandoned buildings, burned-out cars. Gone and replaced by something beautiful.

The sound of the ocean, Sarah and her under-stocked community center. Bethanne awash with floral prints and no customers.

The two places were becoming meshed into one. He was obviously losing his mind.

"Cab?"

"Sorry? I'm not sure . . ." *About anything.*

"There's a hang-up with the bridge between the A Tower and B Tower."

Cab dragged his attention to the end of Tony's pencil point.

"What kind of hang-up?"

"Some jackass in the zoning office is saying that this isn't within the limits of the town ordinance. Or something."

"I'm on it," Frank said. "But we might want to think about moving it down a couple of levels."

"I thought this was all cleared with the zoning board," Cab snapped.

Frank and Tony flinched.

Under the table, Bailey's foot rubbed along his calf. Warning him to cool it.

"Sorry, I've had a long weekend." God, he was like Pavlov's dog. He didn't need Bailey to ride herd on his temper. This was the kind of thing that should have been cleared before they got to this stage of development. Someone had dropped the ball. He had every right to be pissed.

"So can we move it down to the third floor?"

"The point was to allow direct access from the one spa floor to the other so there wouldn't be service repetition. If you move it down, why not just let them walk outside in that case?"

"The point is to keep them from having to go outside."

In a beach resort. Right. God forbid someone would actually have to breathe the salt air. Because they had a whole air-purifying system for each residential and business tower.

"You guys can work out the details," George said, reaching into his wallet. He pulled out a credit card, which he handed to the waiter who had appeared in the doorway. "I want to start demolition next week. We'll adapt as we go."

"George, a lot of people are still living in those blocks."

"There are always a few holdouts. They'll move soon enough once we bring the bulldozers in."

"Some of them must own their own homes."

"They were the first in line. Nothing like a little financial incentive to get them packing up."

Cab shook his head. *Little, right.* Like Silas. "Are they being relocated? Where are they going to go?"

"Not our problem. They were given plenty of notice."

Frank began rolling up the spec sheet but stopped. "Jeez, Cab. You know there's always a bit of collateral damage on these projects. You never bothered about relocation before."

"I've never visited a site before it was cleared."

"Oh, man," said Tony. "You're not goin' all righteous on us, are you?"

"He's goin' home and straight to bed," Bailey said, diffusing the situation. She stood. "He's dead tired. I shouldn't've let you fellas drag us out when he just walked in the door. He'll see ya'll tommorah."

She smiled at the three men, who had stood when she had. Turned her smile on Cab. Was she really making excuses for him? Couldn't he make his own excuses . . . if he needed them?

Is this what his life would be? With Bailey navigating the waters of business and society, pulling him along behind her.

Cab stood. "Sorry, guys. I'm beat. And can't really think clearly. I'll look into it tomorrow."

THEY HAD BARELY gotten in the car when Bailey turned on him. "What is wrong with you? This is a huge project. Do you really want to upset George? He can get vindictive. Daddy's known him forever and told me to keep you on his good side. He can make or break your career."

"You know. I hadn't seen my uncle in a good fifteen years. That was wrong. I should have given back to him for all he did for me. But I didn't."

"I'm sure he understood."

"I'm sure he did, too. It doesn't make it right."

They drove in silence for a while.

"Everything is broken down there. The carousel building, his house; hell, most of the town. But the beach is rebuilding, half the town is on their way up."

"Mmm."

"He'd closed up the carousel and stored the animals. He was saving them for me."

"How sweet of him."

"The center of town used to be that carousel. It was hard for me to see what's happened to it. The building, the carousel itself. Well, it could be fixed with a lot of work. When I saw that empty platform, I was sure he'd sold them off, but he hadn't."

"Well, now you can sell them off. Luanne Strickler has one in her lake house. She paid something like twenty thousand for it. I mean it's cute and all. But twenty thousand? I'd rather put it into a honeymoon."

He pulled into the garage, and they went upstairs. They didn't speak on their way upstairs. But he could tell her mind was elsewhere.

And so was his.

And in the same way an elusive piece of design suddenly falls into place, and the whole structure makes sense, the thing Cab had been missing fell into place.

As soon as they were inside the apartment, he said, "I want you to go to Stargazey with me."

"Oh, Cab, honey, you know I'd love to, but there are so many things to do. And you just got back. Maybe next summer."

"No, I mean I want to move there."

Her eyelashes fluttered once, then she stared.

The silence stretched while he waited for her to absorb his meaning.

"Have you lost your mind? It's hours away. How are you going to manage that commute? 'Cause if you think you're goin' to stay in town Monday through Friday and have me waiting patiently for you to come home on the weekends, you can think again."

"I mean, move there permanently. I helped mend a piece of porch rail this afternoon. Do you know how long it's been since I actually did something with my hands?"

"Well, that's the whole point isn't it? Hire people to do it for you, so you won't have to?"

"No. That was never the point. The design was the point. But I didn't expect this total disconnect between the plan and the people. I wasn't even aware of it until this weekend."

"You're sounding like some lunatic agitator."

"I'm going to run a carousel, my uncle's carousel."

They locked eyes. She didn't believe him. How could she? She had no way of understanding what he needed. It would never make sense to her. That was his fault as much as hers. She wouldn't be going to live in Stargazey with him. That didn't fit into her plan. And he couldn't fit in it, either. Not anymore. He knew they would both be miserable if he stayed here.

"Just think about it."

"There's nothing to think about."

"I'm telling them I'm off the project. I'm leaving the firm."

A flush spread over her chest and into her face. "Then you'll go without me." She pouted and gave him the sultry look that she always used to get her way. And he could see that she thought she had won.

She was wrong. They were wrong. Had always been wrong. Cab just hadn't seen it or didn't want to see it. It was hard to admit that he'd been the arm candy rather than the other way around.

She cared more about her life and lifestyle than she did about him, and he cared more about his future than he cared about her. There was bound to be heartache if they tried to make it work.

"I'm sorry, Bailey. I changed the rules, I didn't mean to. But it happened. This is something I have to do, want to do. People are counting on me."

"Then go by all means. I give you two weeks before you get tired of playing Peter Pan and realize what a mistake you've made. So let me know when you come to your senses and decide to grow up. I'll see if I'm still available."

She grabbed her purse and keys and walked to the door. "I'll send someone over to get my things next week."

"Bailey."

She waited, waited for him to capitulate, but it was too late.

"I'm sorry."

Those sultry eyes grew cold as diamond. "Peter Pan." The door didn't slam behind her. The hinges were designed so it wouldn't make noise.

Cab poured himself another drink, but he put it on the table untouched. He felt guilty but relieved. Really relieved. It was an awful way to break things off, but at least they wouldn't end up living in a hateful marriage.

And he realized that his life, the one he was meant to live, had been changed years before, when he'd fallen in love, not with Bailey, but with Stargazey Point.

Maybe he was Peter Pan. Maybe he would hate living in Stargazey Point, alone. But not trying was not an option. He would just have to wait and see.

He looked around his apartment, realized there was nothing he would miss and nothing to keep him here any longer.

He retrieved his suitcase out of the closet, added

a larger one to it, and packed all the clothes that would fit.

He'd have to come back. He'd have to make it square with the firm. Finish up whatever projects they wanted long-distance, but not the Myrtle Beach complex. He'd probably have to make trips back here, that was okay as long as he had a home to return to. A home in Stargazey Point.

When his bags were filled, he rolled them out of the apartment and set the lock. It was pitch-black when he drove out of Atlanta, but the sun was rising as he drove into Stargazey Point.

ERVINA ROLLED OVER on the mattress, opened one eye to the rising sun. Laughed. It was gonna be a mighty fine day.

Want to know what happens next for Cab, the carousel, and the woman who steals his heart? Keep reading for a sneak peek at

STARGAZEY POINT

Prologue

EVEN WHEN THE CAROUSEL MUSIC slowly wobbled to silence, Cab could still hear it playing inside his head. Sometimes he heard it in his dreams, and he and Midnight Lady would gallop over the sand, wild like the wind—his uncle Ned had read that from a book once, *wild like the wind*.

His uncle locked up the carousel, stuck the cash box under his arm, and came to stand beside him. "Tired, son?"

"No, sir," Cab said, stifling a yawn.

"It's a mighty fine night, ain't it?"

Cab nodded. Stargazey Point was just about the best place in the world. Like living in a carnival.

Uncle Ned said good night to the women closing up the community store. They were going home for the night, but out on the pier people played the arcades and ate cotton candy and drank lemonade. If he listened real hard, Cab could hear music coming from the pavilion out at the end, where the grown-ups would be dancing to a real live band.

Ned put his arm around Cab's shoulders. "Time we were getting home. Have us some leftover bar-becue and get to bed."

They walked away from the beach, the lights, and the sounds and into the night. They were halfway home when Uncle Ned stopped in the middle of the dark street. "Look up at the sky, Cab."

Cab did. The sky was black and there were more stars than you could ever count. He sighed. School would be starting soon, and he'd have to leave his uncle for another year. He didn't want to go; he didn't like boarding school, and everyone here was nice.

"I wish I could stay in Stargazey Point forever."

"Maybe you will one day. It's a magical place, sure enough. It can mend your heart, make you strong, and show you the way to follow your dream. You remember that, Cab. There's not a better place in the whole world than right here at the Point."

Chapter 1

HATE. HOW MANY TIMES A day did that word come up in conversation. *I hate these shoes with this outfit. I hate Jell-O with fruit.* People laugh and say *I hate it when that happens.* Hate could be a joke. Or an all-consuming fire that singed your spirit before eating your soul.

Abbie Sinclair had seen it in all its forms. Okay, maybe not all, and for that she was thankful, but in too many forms to process, to turn a cold eye, to keep plugging away in spite of it all.

A sad commentary on someone who had just turned thirty. Somehow, Abbie thought that the big three-oh would set her free, leave the crushed, dispirited twenties behind. But as the therapist told her during her first session, she wouldn't be able to go forward until she came to terms with her past.

She didn't go back—to the therapist or the past.

So here she was five thousand feet above Indiana, Kentucky, or some other state on her way from Chicago to South Carolina, thinking about hate instead of worrying about what to have for dessert instead of Jell-O or what shoes *would* go with this outfit.

Abbie knew she had to jettison her hate or it would destroy her. But no matter how many times she'd written the word, torn the paper into little strips, shredded it, burned it, ran water over it until it disintegrated, stepped on it—no matter how many times she'd symbolically thrown it away, forced it out of her heart—there seemed to be just a little left, and it would grow back, like pus in an infected wound.

Pus? Really? Had she really just made that analogy? Abbie pressed her fingers to her temples. The absolute lowest. Purple prose. Bad writing and ineffective emotion, something her mentor and lover insisted had no place in cutting-edge documentaries. Something her post-flower-child mother insisted had no place anywhere in life. And something that her best friend, Celeste, said was just plain tacky.

Besides, it didn't come close to what she really felt.

Abbie had been full of fire when she started out. She'd planned to expose the evils of the world, do her part in righting injustice, make people understand and change. The Sinclairs' youngest daughter would finally join the ranks of her do-gooding family. Instead, that fire had turned inward and was destroying her. How arrogant and naive she had been. How easily she'd lost hope.

"Don't be so hard on yourself," Celeste said when Abbie showed up at her apartment with one jungle-rotted duffel bag and a bucketful of tears. "You can probably get your old job back. Want me to ask?"

Abbie just wanted to sleep, except with sleep came dreams peopled by the dead, asking why, why, why of the living.

They decided what she needed was a change of scene. At least that's what Celeste decided. Somewhere comfortable with people who were kind. Celeste knew just the place. With her relatives in a South Carolina beach town named Stargazey Point.

"You'll like it there," Celeste said. "And you'll love Aunt Marnie and Aunt Millie and Uncle Beau. They're really my great or maybe it's my great-great . . . but they're sweethearts and they'd love to have you."

It did sound good: quiet, peace, sun, and surf. "I'll go," Abbie said.

She was a basket case. She needed therapy. She went on vacation instead.

Celeste drove her to O'Hare. "You'll have to take a cab from the airport. I don't think they drive any-more. It'll take about forty minutes if there's no traffic and costs about sixty dollars. Here." She thrust a handful of bills at Abbie then tried to take her coat. "You won't need it there."

Abbie refused the money and clung to her coat; she didn't need it. That burning emotion she couldn't kill was enough to keep her warm on the coldest day.

There was a mini bottle of unopened chardonnay on the tray table before her. She was still clutching her coat.

She wasn't ordinarily a slow learner. And she usually didn't run. That had changed in a heartbeat. And that's when the hate rushed in.

She hated the company whose arrogance had washed away an entire schoolroom of children and the boy and his donkey, hated the security people who had smashed their cameras, hated those who stood by and watched or ran in terror, who dragged her away when she was only trying to save someone, anyone. Those who arrested Werner and threw him in a jail where he met with an "unfortunate accident."

For that she hated them most of all. Selfish, but there it was. They had killed Werner on top of everything else.

And there was not a damn thing she could do about it. There was no footage, no Werner; she'd barely escaped before they confiscated her visa. Others weren't so lucky.

The tears started, but she forced them back. How

could she allow herself tears when everyone else had suffered more?

"SHE SHOULD BE here any minute now, Sister, and you haven't gotten out the tea service. Do you think it's goin' to polish itself? And look how you're dressed."

Marnie Crispin glanced down at her dungarees and the old white T-shirt that Beau had put out for the veterans' box, then looked at her younger sister and sighed. Millie was dressed in a floral print shirt-waist that had to be twenty years old but was pressed like it had just come off the rack at Belks Department Store.

"I know how I'm dressed; the garden doesn't weed itself. I'm planning to change. And I'm not getting out the tea service."

"But, Sister."

"You don't want to scare the girl away, do you?"

"No," said Millie, patting at the white wisps of hair that framed her thin face. "But she's come all the way from Chicago, poor thing. And I want everything to be just perfect for her. Beau, you're droppin' shavings all over my carpet."

Their younger brother, who would turn seventy-nine in two months, was sitting in his favorite chintz-covered chair, the ubiquitous block of wood and his pocketknife in hand. He looked down at his feet and the curls of wood littered there.

"Oh." He attempted to push them under the chair with the side of his boot.

"How many times have I told you not to drop shavings on my carpet?"

Beau rocked forward and pushed himself to his feet.

"Where do you think you're going?"

Beau looked down at the carving in his hand, back at Millie. "Going to watch out for that taxicab from the front porch."

Millie pursed her lips, but there was no rancor in it. Beau was Beau and they loved him. "Just you mind you don't drop shavings all over my porch."

Beau shuffled out of the room.

"And tuck that shirttail in," Millie called after him.

CABOT REYNOLDS HEARD the car go by. They didn't get much sightseeing this time of year, a few fishermen, an occasional antiquer, a handful of die-hard sun worshippers, though most of them preferred the more upscale hotels of Myrtle Beach.

There were a few year-round residents and hearing a car wasn't all that unusual. In the year he'd lived here, he'd come to recognize the characteristic sound of just about every car, truck, and motorcycle in the area. And he didn't recognize the one that had just passed. Which could only mean one thing.

Wiping his hands on a well-used chamois, he

climbed over the engine housing and looked out between the broken lattice of the window. Whoever it was had come and gone.

He tossed the chamois on his worktable, lifted his keys off the peg by the door, and stopped to look around as he did at the end of every workday. For a full minute he just stood and breathed in the faint odor of machine oil, mildew, and childhood memories.

He tried to imagine the time when he'd stop for the day, look up, and see all the work he'd put into the old derelict building gleaming back at him; the colored lights refracting off the restored mirrors bursting into fractured reds, blues, and yellows, while music swirled around his head and the smell of fresh sawdust curled in his nostrils.

So far he only saw a dark almost empty room, locked away from the world by a sagging plywood door. Right now he only saw how much more there was to do. But never once since he'd returned had he ever looked over the space and thought, *What the hell have I done?*

Cabot padlocked the door, then crossed the street to Hadley's, the local grocery store, bait shop, and gas station. He jogged up the wooden steps to the porch and was just pulling a Coke out of the old metal ice chest when Silas Cook came out the door, a string bag of crabs slung over his shoulder. He dropped the bag into a bucket of water and sat down on the steps. Cab sat down beside him and took a long swig from the bottle of Coke.

"You see that taxicab drive through town awhile back?" Silas asked.

"I heard it. Did you?"

"Sure did. Me and Hadley came right out here on the porch and watched it drive by."

"See the passenger?"

"A girl come all the way from Chicag-ah."

Cabot nodded. Like Chicago was the end of the earth.

"You goin' on over there?" asked Silas, nodding down the street toward the old Crispin House.

"After I get cleaned up. I finagled myself an invitation to dinner."

"Well, you in luck there, 'cause I just dropped off a dozen of the finest lady blue claws you'll see this season. Told Ervina she oughta just drop em in the pot but Miss Millie, she want crab bisque. So she make crab bisque."

Cabot leaned back and rested his elbows on the top step. "Fine dining and a chance to get a good, close look at the Crispins' guest. Find out just what she's up to."

"What do you think she's up to? She's a friend of their niece's, like they said, come on vacation."

"Maybe. But what do we know about their niece? They haven't seen her in years. Maybe she sees a gold mine waiting to be exploited."

Silas pushed to his feet and looked down at Cab. "Go on, Mr. Cab. You don't trust much of nobody, do you?"

Cabot was taken aback. "Why do you say that? I trust you, and Hadley, and Beau and . . ."

"I mean other people."

"Sure I do."

"You more protective of this town than folks who've lived here all their lives, and their daddies and granddaddies, too."

"You gotta protect what's yours, you should know that, Silas."

"Yessuh, I know it. And I learnt it the hard way. I just don't get why you know it. Well, I'd best be getting these gals in my own pot." Silas started down the steps; when he got to the bottom, he turned back to Cabot. "You tell Mr. Beau, I'm going out fishin' tomorrah if he wanna come."

"I will." Cabot gave the older man a quick salute and finished his Coke while he watched Silas walk down the street. Then he went inside to pay for his drink.

"One Co-cola," Hadley said, punching the keys of an ancient cash register. "You see Silas outside?"

"Yeah," Cab said. "I'm getting crab bisque at the Crispins' tonight."

"Did he also tell you we seen their visitor?"

"Yep."

"She was a pretty thing as far as I could see. Pale

as a ghost though, even her hair, kinda whitelike. She looked out of the window just as she passed by and I swear it was like she looked right into me. It was kinda spooky."

"Spooky or speculative? Like someone planning to cheat the Crispins out of their house and land?"

"Don't know about that. Silas says they're expecting her. Friend of their great-niece's or some such."

"Maybe," Cabot agreed. "I'll keep an eye on her."

"Know you will, son. Know you will."

Cabot walked home, thinking about the Crispins and his uncle Ned, who was the reason he was here. Or at least the reason that brought him to Stargazey Point this last time. Ned had died and left Cabot everything.

He'd hardly seen his uncle since he'd graduated from high school over fifteen years ago. But before that, he'd spent every summer with Ned, working long hours at the now defunct boardwalk.

He'd driven over from Atlanta to settle Ned's estate. It wasn't much, the old octagonal building, a small tin-roofed cottage in the backside of town. And the contents of a shed situated inland and watched over by an ancient Gullah man named Abraham.

That discovery had sealed his fate. The memories of the magical summers he'd spent with Ned broke through the high-pressured, high-tech world he inhabited, and he knew he had to recapture that magic. He gave up his "promising" career as an industrial architect for an uncertain future. Traded his minimalist-designed, state-of-the-art apartment for a rotten porch, broken windows, and peeling paint.

According to his Atlanta colleagues, he'd lost his mind.

When he asked his fiancée, Bailey, to move to Stargazey Point with him, she accused him of playing Peter Pan. Just before she threw her two-karat engagement ring at his head.

Peter Pan or crazy, he didn't care. He was working longer hours than he had in Atlanta, but he fell into bed each night and slept like a baby until sunrise. Woke up each morning with a clear conscience and he felt alive.

Things had changed in the years since he'd visited here as a boy. People had been hit hard. Houses sat empty, where their owners had given up and sold out or just moved on. All around them, real estate was being gobbled up by investors.

Silas was right; he didn't trust people. Especially ones who came with big ideas on how to improve their little, mostly forgotten town—starting with selling all your property to them. He knew those people; hell, he'd been one of those people.

And now suddenly, out of the blue, a friend of the niece shows up, which was a stretch considering they hadn't seen their great-niece in years. He'd tried to convince the Crispins not to let her stay in the house. They knew nothing about her; she might have ulterior motives and he'd be damned if he'd let those three be taken advantage of. They were proud, old-fashioned, and close to penniless. Vulnerable to any scam.

Abbie Sinclair. Just the name sounded like pencil skirts and four-inch heels. A calfskin briefcase attached to a slender hand with perfectly manicured fingernails, talons just waiting to snatch away their home and way of life.

ABBIE SHOULD HAVE seen it coming once the taxi entered the tunnel of antebellum oak trees. One second she'd been looking at the ocean, the next the sun disappeared and they bounced along uneven ground beneath an archway of trees. The temperature dropped several degrees, and Abbie's eyes strained against the sudden darkness to see ahead. Another minute and they were spit out into the sunshine again.

And there was Crispin House.

It was more than a house, more like a Southern plantation. Not the kind with big white columns, but three-storied white wood and stucco, with wraparound porches on the upper two floors. The first floor was supported by a series of stone arches that made Abbie think of a monastery with dark robed monks going about their daily chores in the shadows. Italianate, if she remembered her architectural styles correctly.

The taxi stopped at the steps that led up to the front door. For a long minute Abbie just sat in the backseat of the cab and stared.

"Whooo." The driver whistled. "Somebody sure needs to give that lady a coat of paint."

He was right. The house had been sorely neglected. She just hoped the inside was in better shape.

She could see spots of peeling paint and a few unpainted balusters where someone had repaired the porch rail. There was a patch of uneven grass and one giant solitary oak that spread its branches over the wide front steps, casting the porch in shadow.

This was crazy. Celeste had merely said her relatives would love to have her stay with them, they had plenty of room. She hadn't said that they could have housed a large portion of the Confederate army. Well, she'd stay one night and if things didn't work out, she'd seen an inn in the little town they'd just driven through. It at least had a coat of paint.

She paid the driver, added a generous tip since it seemed that he wouldn't have any return fares, and prepared to meet the Crispin family.

There was movement on the porch, and Abbie realized that a man had been sitting on the rail watching her. He stood, fumbled in his pockets, brushed his palms together, and started down the stairs, lean

and lanky and moving slow, his knees sticking out
to the side with each downward step.

Abbie reached for the door handle, but the door
opened and a face appeared in the opening. His
skin was crinkled and deeply lined from the sun.
A shock of thick white hair had escaped from
his carefully groomed part and stuck up above
his forehead. Bright blue eyes twinkled beneath
bushy white eyebrows and managed to appear
both fun loving and wise at the same time. Abbie
suspected he'd been quite handsome as a young
man. He still was.

"Miz Sinclair?"

"Yes," Abbie said, though it took her a second
to recognize her own name. In its slow delivery, it
sounded more like Sinclayuh. It was soft and me-
lodious, like a song, and Abbie relaxed just a little.
"You must be Mr. Crispin."

"Yes'm, that's me. But folks round here all call
me Beau." He held out a large bony hand, the veins
thick as ropes across the back, then he snatched it
back, rubbed it vigorously on his pants leg, and pre-
sented it again.

Abbie smiled up at Beauregard Crispin, took his
proffered hand, and got out of the car.

The driver carried her two bags up to the porch.
"Y'all have a nice stay," he said, then nodded to Mr.
Crispin, got back in the taxi, and drove away.

Abbie felt a moment of panic. She had a feeling there might not be another taxi for miles.

"After you."

She hesitated, just looking at Beau's outstretched hand, then she forced a smile and began to climb the wide wooden steps. She'd just reached the porch when the screen door opened and two women stepped out of the rectangle of darkness. They had to be Millie and Marnie. The Crispin sisters.

Here's the thing about my relatives, Celeste had told her. *They're sweet as pie, but they're old-fashioned. I mean really old-fashioned, like pre–Civil War old-fashioned.*

Abbie had laughed, well, her version of a laugh these days. *I get it, they're old-fashioned. No four-letter words, no politics, no religion. Not to worry, I have better sense than to talk politics to people who lost the wahr.*

The what?

The war. That was my attempt at a Southern accent. No good?

Celeste shook her head. *Not by a long shot.* She dropped into a speech pattern that she'd nearly erased through much practice and four years of studying communications. *The wahuh. Two syllables and soft. It's South Carolina, not Texas. We're refined. We've got Charleston.*

Abbie impulsively grabbed Celeste's hand. *Don't you want to go with me?*

I'd love to but I can't get away from the station.

When was the last time you had a vacation?

Can't remember. You know the media. Out of sight, out of— Go have a good time. Let them pamper you. They're experts.

Now, Abbie suddenly got it. She would have recognized them in a crowd. Millie, the younger sister, prim, petite, neatly dressed and hair coifed in a tidy little bun at the nape of her neck. And Marnie, taller, rawboned, dressed in a pair of dungarees and a tattered man's T-shirt smeared with dirt. Her white hair was thick and wild with curls. According to Celeste, Marnie had left the fold at sixteen only to return fifty years later, the intervening years unspoken of, what she had done or where she had been, a mystery.

Us kids used to make up stories about her. Once we were convinced she was a spy for the CIA, then we decided she traveled to Paris and became the mistress of a tortured painter and posed nude for him. We were very precocious.

She came for a visit once, but we weren't allowed to see her. She only stayed two days, and I heard Momma tell Daddy that she was drinking buttermilk the whole time she was there, 'cause it was the only thing she missed. And Daddy said, it was because it covered the smell of the scotch she poured into it.

They're teetotalers.

Not at all. Aunt Millie has a sherry every afternoon.

"My de-ah," Millie Crispin said, coming forward and holding out both hands. "Welcome to Crispin

House. We're so glad to have you. Beau, get Abbie's luggage and bring it inside."

"Please, I can—" But that was as far as she got before she was swept across the threshold by the deceptively fragile-looking Millie.

"Now you just come inside and leave everything to Beau."

Abbie didn't want to think of Beau struggling with her suitcases, but she saw Marnie slip past them to give her brother a hand, just before Millie guided her through a wide oak door and into a high-ceilinged foyer.

"I thought you might like to see your room first and get settled in," Millie said in her soft drawl.

"Thank you." Abbie followed her up a curved staircase to the second floor, matching her steps to Millie's slower ones.

At the top of the stairs was a landing that overlooked the foyer. A portrait of a man in uniform hung above a side table and large Chinese vase. Three hallways led to the rest of the house.

Millie started down the center hall. "We've put you in the back guest suite. Celeste and her mama and daddy used to stay there when they visited." Millie sighed. "There's a lovely view." She chattered on while Abbie followed a footstep behind her and tried to decipher the pattern of the faded oriental runner.

They came to the end of the hall and Millie

opened a door. "Here we are. I hope you like everything." They stepped inside to a large darkened room. A row of wooden shutters blocked the light from the windows and a set of French doors that Abbie hoped led to a balcony. Millie hurried over to the windows and opened the shutters. Slices of sunlight poured in, revealing an elegant but faded loveseat and several chairs.

"Over here is your bedroom," Millie said, guiding Abbie through another door to another room, this one fitted out with a high four-poster bed with the same shuttered door and windows. Millie bustled about the room opening the shutters and pointing out amenities. "The bath's through there . . ."

Millie's words buzzed about Abbie's ears. She appreciated her desire to be welcoming, but she wanted—needed—solitude, anonymity, not someone hovering solicitously over her every second. Coming here had been a big mistake.

"If you need anything, anything at all, you just pull that bell pull and Ervina will come see to you."

Ervina? Was there another sister Celeste hadn't told her about?

"You just make yourself at home. We generally have dinner at six, but come down any time you like."

Abbie followed her back into the sitting room and to the door. "Now you have a rest and then we'll have a nice visit." Millie finally stepped into the hallway.

Abbie shut the door on Millie's smile and leaned against it.

There was a tap behind her that made Abbie jump away from the door. *Be patient,* she told herself. *She's trying to be nice.* She opened the door.

Marnie was there with her suitcases. Abbie opened the door wider and Marnie lugged them in. She was followed by an even older African American woman carrying a tray.

"You shouldn't have carried my bags."

"No bother. We send the luggage up on a dumb-waiter. Ervina, put that tray over on the Hepple-white."

Ervina wasn't a sister. She was the servant. And she was ancient.

Ervina shuffled into the room, carrying a tray laden with cups, saucers, and plates of food that looked heavier than the woman who carried it. Abbie felt a swell of outrage and fought not to take the load from the woman.

Marnie walked through the room turning on several lamps. "We'll leave you alone. Millie insisted on the tray. Don't overeat because she's going to feed you again in a couple of hours. And don't worry that you'll be trapped in the house listening to two old broads talk your ear off. You just do however you want. Come, Ervina, let's leave the poor girl alone." Marnie headed for the door.

Ervina followed. She slanted a look at Abbie as

she passed by, nodded slowly as if Abbie had just met her expectations, then she shuffled through the door and shut it without a backward look.

Bemused, Abbie turned off the lamps Marnie had just turned on. They had to be conserving electricity. Because from the little she'd seen of Crispin House, shabby genteel wasn't just a lifestyle, it was a necessity.

And then there was the elaborate tea tray, sterling silver, filled with cakes and little sandwiches with the crusts cut off, tea in a bone china pot and a pitcher of lemonade.

"Celeste, I could brain you. What the hell have you gotten me into?"

Abbie took a cucumber sandwich and crossed to the French doors. After fumbling one handed with the handle, she popped the rest of the little sandwich in her mouth and used both hands to pull the doors open.

She stepped out to the wraparound porch where several white rocking chairs and wicker side tables were lined up facing the ocean. The air was tangy with salt, and she breathed deeply before crossing to the rail.

Below her a wide lawn slid into white dunes that dipped and billowed before the old mansion like a crinoline. Delicate tufts of greenery embroidered the way to the beach, wide and white and ending in a point that stretched like a guiding finger to the horizon.

And beyond that, water and sky. She'd come to the edge of the world. Not a violent wave-crashing, jagged-rock edge that you'd expect, but the Southern genteel version with fat lazy waves rolling in, tumbling one over the other before spilling into white foam on the sand.

Abbie filled her lungs with the spicy, clean air and slowly let it out. Part of her tension oozed away. She was tempted just to stay right there looking at the ocean forever, but they were expecting her for dinner.

She went inside to unpack. Her coat was lying across the chenille bedspread.

Her cell phone rang. She turned her back on the coat and checked caller ID.

"Perfect timing," she said, answering it.

"Did you just arrive?" Celeste's voice crackled at the other end of the call. Great. Lousy cell reception. Well, she wanted solitude.

"A few minutes ago. This place is incredible, kind of Southern gothic."

"Ugh. Is it in really bad shape? I've been meaning to get back, but I never seem to find the time."

"The outside more than the interior, though it looks like someone has started repairs. But everything is very comfortable, the sisters are a hoot, and Beau . . . I adore him already."

"Which room did they give you?"

"One with peach paint that opens onto the veranda and a view of the ocean. Why didn't you tell me about the beach?"

"I did."

"Oh, well, it's incredible. I haven't had a chance to go down yet, but I plan to spend tomorrow laying out. Thank you."

"No prob. Don't forget your sunscreen. It isn't hot yet, but the sun can burn. Especially with your skin."

"Thanks, Ma."

"Oh, hell, I know you know more about sunburn than I do, considering the sun hardly ever creeps into my office." Celeste sighed. "I'm kind of envious."

"Then why don't you try to get away? It's really quite wonderful," Abbie said. And her stay here would be easier to handle with Celeste to deflect some of the attention.

"I wish. I told you it was just what you needed. You have to promise to soak up some rays for me."

"I will, and you were right. Even if I had to fall apart to realize it."

"Don't think about that. You'll get back into it—when you're ready."

And nobody, not even Abbie, thought she would ever be ready. She knew she could never go back. Back had been torn away from her. Back was no longer an option.

"Hey, listen, I have a very important question for you."

"Yes?"

Abbie could hear the wariness in her friend's voice. "Am I expected to dress for dinner?"

Celeste laughed. It was a sound that made Abbie feel homesick.

"Well, I haven't been there in years, but it is Sunday dinner."

"I take that to mean yes. But how dressed?"

"You know, just nice, a dress, not too short, maybe some pearls."

"Got it. I'd better get hopping. I don't want to be late. And Celeste. Thanks. I take it back, all that stupid stuff I said. You were right. This is just what I needed."

Chapter 2

ABBIE HALF EXPECTED A GONG to announce dinner. But when it didn't ring at a quarter to six, she knew she couldn't hide in her room any longer. She'd dressed in her any-occasion black dress and softened it with a string of faux pearls and a short floral jacket that she'd picked up on the sale rack at Marshall Fields. She opted for sandals and prayed that the sisters wouldn't be waiting for her in chiffon hostess gowns.

She managed to find her way to the parlor where the Crispins were sipping amber liquid from small glasses. The sherry Celeste had told her about.

Millie, dressed in light green, sat on the edge of a delicate upholstered chair, her skirts spread about her like an octogenarian Scarlett O'Hara. Marnie was sitting on the couch, legs crossed. She'd changed into a pair a navy blue slacks and a silky blouse covered in a blue hyacinth pattern.

Beau, wearing a dark suit and looking uncomfortable, stood up when Abbie stepped through the archway. And so did another man.

"Abbie, come in and sit down over here," said Millie. "Beau, pour Abbie a little glass of sherry."

"She might prefer something else, Sister," Marnie said.

"Oh." Millie's hand flew to her chest. "Of course." She frowned at Abbie, more flustered than judgmental.

"Sherry's fine," Abbie said. She could swear Marnie snorted. Abbie took a closer look at Marnie's sherry glass and wondered if it might contain the infamous scotch.

The stranger had sat down and was lounging in a big club chair, one ankle crossed over his knee. He was drinking something dark in a tumbler. It matched his attitude and his looks, which were pretty okay even by Chicago standards. Dark hair, dark eyes, tanned, fit from what she could tell by the shirt front that showed through his unbuttoned sports jacket. He eyed her speculatively and not at all friendly.

Good. For a minute she'd been afraid the sisters were trying to set her up.

"My goodness, where are my manners," Millie

said. "Cabot, this is our guest, Abbie Sinclair. Abbie, this is Cabot Reynolds . . . the third."

The third, right. Abbie fought not to roll her eyes; Marnie didn't bother.

"How do you do?" he said dryly.

"Nice to meet you," she said, matching his tone. The air between them could have chilled lemonade. Fine by Abbie.

"And how long are you staying, Miss Sinclair?"

Longer than you want me to, obviously, thought Abbie. And what was that all about? She thought Southern men were supposed to have impeccable manners. But maybe he wasn't totally Southern. His voice modulated from a soft Southern drawl to something with more bite. Probably educated at a stuffy private school, where Reynolds the first and second had attended.

At that moment a gong echoed from somewhere in the house.

Marnie shook her head and stood up. They walked across the hall to the dining room. Cabot the third escorted Millie; Beau offered an elbow first to Abbie, then Marnie.

Marnie leaned past her brother. "Don't get used to all this grandeur," she whispered. "Usually we just eat on trays in front of the television."

Abbie smiled. "Good to know." Whatever this trip would be, Abbie was getting the feeling it wouldn't be dull. The three siblings alone would make a great study. Gentility gone to seed, but struggling to survive. A way of life, fragile and soon to become extinct . . .

Abbie's step faltered as her mind automatically switched into documentary mode. Beau's hand tightened over hers, and he gave her an encouraging smile. She smiled back and with an effort pulled her mind back to dinner.

No more lapses like that, she warned herself. That life was over. She wouldn't go there again.

The dining room was a long rectangular room painted a pale yellow and surrounded by a white chair rail. At the far end, French doors opened onto a brick patio and overgrown shrubbery. The oval dining table was placed off center, which Abbie surmised was because several leaves had been taken out to accommodate only five diners. It was still huge and she was glad that the place settings had been clustered around one end with Millie at the head of the table, Beau and Marnie to her left, and Cabot and Abbie to her right.

Dinner was everything she had imagined a Southern dinner to be. Crystal wine and water glasses, the good china, and sterling flatware. The house itself might be slowly fading away, but they were still dining in style.

The first course arrived in a flowered goldrimmed soup tureen carried by a young African American man dressed in a white coat and black trousers several inches too short. He held the tureen as if it contained nitroglycerin while Ervina ladled a rich crab bisque, pale pink with chunks of crabmeat, into their bowls.

"Thank you, Ervina," Marnie said. "How are you doing this evening, Jerome?"

Jerome grinned at her for a second before he lowered his head. "Fine, ma'am," he mumbled and sped back to the kitchen. Ervina followed at a slower pace.

The soup was thick and rich, and Abbie was stuffed by the time the first course arrived. She hadn't been eating very much lately. She looked apprehensively at the roasted chicken, the potatoes, greens of some variety, corn bread, and several other dishes. And she wondered how she could manage to eat enough not to appear rude.

"Why, Millie, this is a feast fit for a king." Cabot the third smiled charmingly at Millie then cut Abbie a sideways look.

"Delicious," she agreed, resenting the arrogant so-and-so who thought he had to prompt her on good manners.

Millie beamed back at the two of them.

Marnie looked across the table and said, "Only eat what you want. It's sometimes hard to eat at the end of a travel day." She aimed the last part of the sentence at Millie.

"Why, of course," said Millie. "And if you get hungry during the night, you just come down to the kitchen and make yourself at home. Ervina goes home at night so you'll have to fend for yourself."

"I'm sure I'll be fine."

"We are early risers and eat breakfast about seven o'clock, but you sleep in and we'll fix you something when you're good and ready."

"Thank you, really. But you don't have to feed me. I'm sure there are plenty of places in town. I'm just happy that you're letting me take advantage of your hospitality."

"Nonsense," Millie said. "We love takin' care of our young people. Though most of them seem to move away as soon as they can. It might be a little dull around here until the season begins, but I'm sure Cabot would love to show you around town."

"Thank you, but—"

"When you're rested up. You'd love to do that, wouldn't you, Cabot?"

Abbie doubted it. "I wouldn't want to take Mr. Reynolds away from . . ." *Whatever it is he does.*

"I'd be happy to." He smiled tightly at Abbie.

She smiled back just as tightly. She'd have to have a talk with the sisters tomorrow and gently, but firmly, tell them she was not interested. Not in Cabot "the third" or anyone else.

"But I can't until Tuesday. The community center's water heater's rusted out and I told Sarah I'd come over and help Otis install the new one. Then I have a job over in Plantersville in the afternoon."

So he worked. As a plumber? Before she could ask him, Jerome came back with individual crystal dishes of a thick yellow pudding filled with chunks of bananas and vanilla wafers.

Abbie managed to eat dessert, which was delicious, listening politely to the conversation without having to think of too much to say. Between the food, and the slow lyrical voices, exhaustion began to creep over her. Millie and Cabot did most of the talking, while Marnie occasionally put in a word or two. Beau just ate, answered when he was spoken to directly, but didn't volunteer any conversation of his own.

A block of partially carved wood sat by his plate, and several times Abbie saw his hand inch toward it only to draw away again at a mere glance from Millie. Abbie wished she had asked more about the family before coming. She knew anecdotal-over-a-martini details, like Marnie camouflaging the smell of scotch with buttermilk, and how Millie ruled the house even though it was really Beau's inheritance. But she hadn't heard any real history, and it was obvious there was some interesting history between the three.

As Abbie watched their interplay, she became more intrigued. She liked the siblings. What she didn't get was how Cabot Reynolds the third fit into it. Celeste hadn't mentioned him. He didn't seem to be a relative, and yet he obviously had free rein of the place. Maybe that's why she was picking up such unfriendliness from him. He was afraid she'd usurp his position as favored guest?

He might be a plumber, but Crispin House and the land that surrounded it must be worth a fortune. And Cabot the third might just be trying to parlay friendship into financial gain—for himself.

Don't get involved, she warned herself. She wasn't going to do that anymore. No more lost causes. No more exposés. No more long weeks of grueling work in hideous conditions just to have your film confiscated, your cameras destroyed, your . . .

"And we want you to stay just as long as you can. If you don't think it will be too dull."

Abbie realized that everyone was looking at her; there was concern on Marnie's face.

God, what had they been talking about? "I don't think it will be dull at all. Solitude is just what I came for."

"Well, you'll find plenty of that here," Marnie said under her breath.

"We won't bother you at all," added Millie. "Will we, Sister?"

"Not at all," Marnie said, attention focused on Abbie. "You just come and go as you like."

Abbie sneaked a peek at Cabot Reynolds. He was frowning at his water glass. He definitely didn't want her around.

Millie stood, and the others took their cue. Beau

surreptitiously slipped the piece of wood in his pocket and edged toward the door.

"I'd best be taking off," Cabot announced as soon as they reached the archway to the parlor. "Your guest looks like she might nod off midsentence."

Abbie widened her eyes and suppressed a yawn.

"By the way, Beau, Silas said he was going fishing tomorrow if you were interested."

"Yes, thank you, Cabot, I think I am. I'll walk you back into town."

"Don't you stay out till all hours," Millie said.

"Haven't stayed out till all hours since I was in the merchant marines," Beau said and winked at Abbie.

"Thank you for dinner," Cab said. "You tell Ervina for me that that's the best crab bisque I had all season."

"I will. Beau, you keep that jacket on if you're going outside."

"G'night, Cab," Marnie said.

Abbie smiled and nodded; Cab nodded. The two men left.

"Well, we won't see him back anytime soon," Millie said with a sigh.

It took Abbie a couple of seconds to realize she was talking about Beau and not Cabot. Beau didn't say much, and he was definitely more comfortable with a piece of wood in his hand than sitting over a china bowl of bisque making polite conversation—

something Abbie could relate to—but he seemed perfectly capable of taking care of himself.

"Would you like to go up to your room, dear? You're welcome to watch some television with Sister and me. We don't have cable, but we can pick up the Charleston and Myrtle Beach stations pretty good."

"I think I'll go up and read for a bit. It must be the salt air, but I'm tired. It was a lovely dinner. Thank you."

"Our pleasure. Good night, dear."

Abbie climbed the stairs to her room, dreading the idea of going to sleep, but dreading the idea of having to watch the evening news with Marnie and Millie more.

She wondered how long she could stand Millie's solicitude. It was probably what Southern hostesses did. Abbie had visited a lot of countries, met all kinds of people, but she'd never met anyone like Millie. It was as if she belonged in another era, like one of those characters in the recent burst of Southern movies. Which, Abbie realized, were probably based on people like Millie.

"I always rely on the kindness of strangers," Abbie mumbled to herself in a pitiful rendition of a Southern accent. And realized she *was* actually relying on the kindness of strangers. And she was grateful.

That night she slept like the dead, and the dead came back to haunt her.

BEAU AND CAB walked back into town. It was a cool evening, growing cooler as the sun sank beneath the horizon, but Beau had shed his suit jacket the minute they were outside and left it hanging on the porch rail.

"You get that engine up and running yet?" Beau asked.

"Not yet, but I'm close," Cab said. "I got it tuned properly and it goes for a few seconds, then it gets hung up. I've scoured rust, oiled parts, refitted pieces, but it still gets hung up."

"I'll come over and take a look for you tomorrow."

"That would be great. Thanks."

Beau nodded. Reached into his pocket for his piece of wood.

"So," Cabot began. "Your visitor seems nice enough."

"Pretty girl," Beau said as he fumbled in his shirt pocket for his knife. "I was always partial to blue-eyed blondes."

Cab groaned inwardly. It wouldn't take much for Abbie Sinclair to have Beau wound around her little finger.

"She's a friend of your niece's?"

"Celeste."

"Right. What did Celeste tell you about her?"

Beau stopped and peered at Cabot. "You interested in her, son?"

"If you mean are we gonna have to fight over her, no."

Beau chuckled.

"She hardly said a word at dinner. I was just curious why she would choose Stargazey Point for a vacation. She looks like an Aruba kind of woman."

"Huh," Beau said. "Don't strike me that way. Something int'resting about her though."

"What?"

"Don't know. But you can feel it."

The only thing Cab felt was trepidation that this was another developer's ploy to cheat the Crispins out of their property. She wouldn't be the first. They'd been circling like buzzards since Cab had been back and probably before then. Silas and a handful of others had sold their property for way below what it was worth, but that was before Cab's return. These days, pretty much everybody came to him for advice. Most of the time he'd tell them not to sell.

It was selfish he knew. Many of them were barely getting by. Hell, he even had to take on some local design jobs, but most of the offers were way below the value of the property.

They reached the old pier and Beau stopped. "You're mighty quiet tonight, boy."

"Got a lot on my mind, I guess."

"Nothin' bad, I hope."

"No, nothing bad." He'd make sure it wasn't. It

was a good thing after all that Millie had coerced him into taking Ms. Sinclair sightseeing. The best thing he could do was to trap her into giving herself away while he was showing her around on Tuesday. And if she did, he'd have her on her way to the airport before she could whistle "Dixie," if she even knew the tune.

"Well, I'll be seeing you tomorrow then." Beau wandered off toward the pier. Cabot watched him climb down the rotting pylons to sit on the cement seawall below. It was still just light enough to see the blade of his knife as it sliced into the unformed block of wood.

Cabot turned toward home thinking about Beau and what it must be like to live surrounded by those two strong-willed women. It would drive Cab mad, but Beau took everything in stride, wandering off to carve beautiful, mysterious forms. Mysterious because Cab had never seen a finished product, not even in all the summers he'd spent here. Maybe Beau never finished them, just carved and whittled until he carved the wood away.

Cab couldn't imagine the Point without Beau and his block of wood.

And he couldn't imagine himself anywhere else.

Instead of going home, he walked the half block to his reason for being in Stargazey. Riffled through his keys until he found the one that opened the padlock that secured the double plywood door. The original doors had been blown off in Hurricane Hugo in 1989, then again in '99 and '04. After the last time, Ned hadn't opened up again. Tourism was off, the beaches had eroded, and with the opening of the big theme parks, there wasn't much call for his kind of business.

Cab pulled at one side of the door. It scraped against the dirt as it arced outward. He'd have to put proper doors on soon—these were too unwieldy and probably not that safe—but he had some time still. He wanted new windows installed, the place painted, the electricity working. . . .

He stepped into the dark cavernous space, thinking he could smell the freshly laid sawdust, hear the distant echo of music, the whirl of lights and mirrors, the delighted squeals of children, the laughter of adults.

Peter Pan? Maybe. He just knew that even with a promising future, a beautiful fiancée, and a substantial stock portfolio, his life had been sterile and bleak. Until he'd come back to Stargazey Point to settle Ned's estate. He'd returned to Atlanta seemingly the same, but he had changed in the space of a few short days and the discovery of Ned's legacy.

He looked into the dark at the strange machinery and half-finished structures and felt happy. He'd given up everything for this, and he'd be damned if he'd let anyone, including Abbie Sinclair, take it away.

Abbie scrambles on her hands and knees. Past the donkey, eyes rolling in terror. She thrusts a rigid arm toward the small hand that stretches open-fingered from the mud. She can't reach it. The harder she tries, the farther it slides away. Only the donkey stays, his head thrashing in the mud. But she can't reach the boy. "I'm sorry, I'm sorry, I'm sorry."

Werner yells at her, she turns. His lips move, but she can't hear him. "What?" she screams. His eyes widen, his arms fly out as his body recoils and blood splatters the air. He falls, slowly, slowly to the ground, calling to her, but she can't hear.

Abbie thrashed against the covers. Sat up. Gasping for breath. It was a dream. The dream. She clutched the sheet as the bed began to shake, move across the floor, the tall posts wavering in the dark, until they disintegrated like ashes around her. She rolled off the bed and crawled toward the French doors across an undulating floor.

Not real, not awake, not real. She grabbed at the door handles, flung the doors wide, and stumbled onto the veranda. She pulled herself up to the balcony rail and peered out to sea. The wind hit her damp skin, and she shivered uncontrollably.

She was in South Carolina with Celeste's family. She was standing on firm wood.

It was dark. Only a lighter aura marked the northern shore where the lights from civilization broke through the night. But straight out to sea was black. And though the stars blinked erratically above her, their light didn't shine on the land.

Abbie crossed her arms over her chest. Closed her eyes and opened them again. She looked up and down the porch, making sure she hadn't wakened the others, not knowing if she'd talked or screamed or cried in her sleep. She heard nothing but the whisper of the waves touching the sand.

This had to stop. She might have awakened one of the Crispins, scared any of the three into a heart attack.

Something creaked in the dark. She whirled around and peered into the shadows. One of the rocking chairs moved slowly back and forth. Abbie backed against the balcony rail. The chair ceased rocking. Hopefully, it was over for tonight.

Just as she began to relax, the chair lurched forward and something clunked to the ground. She froze, felt something rub against her ankles. And then a low rumbling.

It seemed to take forever for her brain to kick into gear. Not a hallucination, not a nightmare. A cat was purring at her feet.

She exhaled so sharply she nearly fell backward.

She knelt down, and the cat bumped against her knee. He, or she, was big and seemed in no hurry to leave. She reached out her hand, and the cat stretched his neck to be stroked.

"Now where did you come from? You're not feral, you're too friendly to be a scavenger, so I'm guessing you're a resident, too."

The cat made a rusty sound that Abbie took as a meow, made a final pass under her hand, and turned to walk slowly and stately, tail twitching, down the veranda. He was swallowed by the darkness long before he reached the end.

Abbie shivered. Her nightshirt was clammy with sweat. She looked quickly around, assuring herself that she was indeed awake. She took a deep breath of salt air, a long last look at the dark, heaving waves, and went back to her room.

She hurried across the carpet and jumped onto the high four-poster, pulled the covers up to her neck. Okay. No one had seen or heard her. And she couldn't be too crazy; the cat liked her. But this couldn't go on. She had to pull herself together.

She'd done her best. She couldn't have done more. She knew that. And yet somehow that wasn't enough. *I'm sorry, I'm sorry, I'm sorry.*

About the Author

SHELLEY NOBLE is a former professional dancer and choreographer. She most recently worked on the films *Mona Lisa Smile* and *The Game Plan*. She is a member of Sisters in Crime, Mystery Writers of America, and Romance Writers of America.